The Defence of Guenevere

AND OTHER POEMS

The Defence of Guenevere

AND OTHER POEMS

WILLIAM MORRIS

ÆGYPAN PRESS

Special thanks to Thierry Alberto, Stephen Blundell and the Online
Distributed Proofreading Team at http://www.pgdp.net.

1908

First Edition, BELL & DALDY, 1858
Reprinted, 1875, for ELLIS & WHITE, and
Subsequently for REEVES & TURNER
Kelmscott Press Edition (revised by the Author), 1892
Transferred to LONGMANS, GREEN, & CO., 1896
New Edition corrected by Kelmscott Press Edition, May 1900
Reprinted January 1908

The Defence of Guenevere and Other Poems
A publication of
ÆGYPAN PRESS

www.aegypan.com

Table of Contents

The Defence of Guenevere

But, knowing now that they would have her speak,
She threw her wet hair backward from her brow,
Her hand close to her mouth touching her cheek,

As though she had had there a shameful blow,
And feeling it shameful to feel ought but shame
All through her heart, yet felt her cheek burned so,

She must a little touch it; like one lame
She walked away from Gauwaine, with her head
Still lifted up; and on her cheek of flame

The tears dried quick; she stopped at last and said:
O knights and lords, it seems but little skill
To talk of well-known things past now and dead.

God wot I ought to say, I have done ill,
And pray you all forgiveness heartily!
Because you must be right, such great lords; still

Listen, suppose your time were come to die,
And you were quite alone and very weak;
Yea, laid a dying while very mightily

The wind was ruffling up the narrow streak
Of river through your broad lands running well:
Suppose a hush should come, then some one speak:

'One of these cloths is heaven, and one is hell,
Now choose one cloth for ever; which they be,
I will not tell you, you must somehow tell

Of your own strength and mightiness; here, see!'
Yea, yea, my lord, and you to ope your eyes,
At foot of your familiar bed to see

A great God's angel standing, with such dyes,
Not known on earth, on his great wings, and hands,
Held out two ways, light from the inner skies

Showing him well, and making his commands
Seem to be God's commands, moreover, too,
Holding within his hands the cloths on wands;

And one of these strange choosing cloths was blue,
Wavy and long, and one cut short and red;
No man could tell the better of the two.

After a shivering half-hour you said:
'God help! heaven's colour, the blue;' and he said, 'hell.'
Perhaps you then would roll upon your bed,

And cry to all good men that loved you well,
'Ah Christ! if only I had known, known, known;'
Launcelot went away, then I could tell,

Like wisest man how all things would be, moan,
And roll and hurt myself, and long to die,
And yet fear much to die for what was sown.

Nevertheless you, O Sir Gauwaine, lie,
Whatever may have happened through these years,
God knows I speak truth, saying that you lie.

Her voice was low at first, being full of tears,
But as it cleared, it grew full loud and shrill,
Growing a windy shriek in all men's ears,

A ringing in their startled brains, until
She said that Gauwaine lied, then her voice sunk,
And her great eyes began again to fill,

Though still she stood right up, and never shrunk,
But spoke on bravely, glorious lady fair!

Whatever tears her full lips may have drunk,

She stood, and seemed to think, and wrung her hair,
Spoke out at last with no more trace of shame,
With passionate twisting of her body there:

It chanced upon a day that Launcelot came
To dwell at Arthur's court: at Christmas-time
This happened; when the heralds sung his name,

Son of King Ban of Benwick, seemed to chime
Along with all the bells that rang that day,
O'er the white roofs, with little change of rhyme.

Christmas and whitened winter passed away,
And over me the April sunshine came,
Made very awful with black hail-clouds, yea

And in the Summer I grew white with flame,
And bowed my head down: Autumn, and the sick
Sure knowledge things would never be the same,

However often Spring might be most thick
Of blossoms and buds, smote on me, and I grew
Careless of most things, let the clock tick, tick,

To my unhappy pulse, that beat right through
My eager body; while I laughed out loud,
And let my lips curl up at false or true,

Seemed cold and shallow without any cloud.
Behold my judges, then the cloths were brought;
While I was dizzied thus, old thoughts would crowd,

Belonging to the time ere I was bought
By Arthur's great name and his little love;
Must I give up for ever then, I thought,

That which I deemed would ever round me move
Glorifying all things; for a little word,
Scarce ever meant at all, must I now prove

Stone-cold for ever? Pray you, does the Lord
Will that all folks should be quite happy and good?
I love God now a little, if this cord

Were broken, once for all what striving could
Make me love anything in earth or heaven?
So day by day it grew, as if one should

Slip slowly down some path worn smooth and even,
Down to a cool sea on a summer day;
Yet still in slipping there was some small leaven

Of stretched hands catching small stones by the way,
Until one surely reached the sea at last,
And felt strange new joy as the worn head lay

Back, with the hair like sea-weed; yea all past
Sweat of the forehead, dryness of the lips,
Washed utterly out by the dear waves o'ercast,

In the lone sea, far off from any ships!
Do I not know now of a day in Spring?
No minute of that wild day ever slips

From out my memory; I hear thrushes sing,
And wheresoever I may be, straightway
Thoughts of it all come up with most fresh sting:

I was half mad with beauty on that day,
And went without my ladies all alone,
In a quiet garden walled round every way;

I was right joyful of that wall of stone,
That shut the flowers and trees up with the sky,
And trebled all the beauty: to the bone,

Yea right through to my heart, grown very shy
With weary thoughts, it pierced, and made me glad;
Exceedingly glad, and I knew verily,

A little thing just then had made me mad;
I dared not think, as I was wont to do,

Sometimes, upon my beauty; If I had

Held out my long hand up against the blue,
And, looking on the tenderly darken'd fingers,
Thought that by rights one ought to see quite through,

There, see you, where the soft still light yet lingers,
Round by the edges; what should I have done,
If this had joined with yellow spotted singers,

And startling green drawn upward by the sun?
But shouting, loosed out, see now! all my hair,
And trancedly stood watching the west wind run

With faintest half-heard breathing sound; why there
I lose my head e'en now in doing this;
But shortly listen: In that garden fair

Came Launcelot walking; this is true, the kiss
Wherewith we kissed in meeting that spring day,
I scarce dare talk of the remember'd bliss,

When both our mouths went wandering in one way,
And aching sorely, met among the leaves;
Our hands being left behind strained far away.

Never within a yard of my bright sleeves
Had Launcelot come before: and now, so nigh!
After that day why is it Guenevere grieves?

Nevertheless you, O Sir Gauwaine, lie,
Whatever happened on through all those years,
God knows I speak truth, saying that you lie.

Being such a lady could I weep these tears
If this were true? A great queen such as I
Having sinn'd this way, straight her conscience sears;

And afterwards she liveth hatefully,
Slaying and poisoning, certes never weeps:
Gauwaine be friends now, speak me lovingly.

Do I not see how God's dear pity creeps
All through your frame, and trembles in your mouth?
Remember in what grave your mother sleeps,

Buried in some place far down in the south,
Men are forgetting as I speak to you;
By her head sever'd in that awful drouth

Of pity that drew Agravaine's fell blow,
I pray your pity! let me not scream out
For ever after, when the shrill winds blow

Through half your castle-locks! let me not shout
For ever after in the winter night
When you ride out alone! in battle-rout

Let not my rusting tears make your sword light!
Ah! God of mercy, how he turns away!
So, ever must I dress me to the fight,

So: let God's justice work! Gauwaine, I say,
See me hew down your proofs: yea all men know
Even as you said how Mellyagraunce one day,

One bitter day in *la Fausse Garde,* for so
All good knights held it after, saw:
Yea, sirs, by cursed unknightly outrage; though

You, Gauwaine, held his word without a flaw,
This Mellyagraunce saw blood upon my bed:
Whose blood then pray you? is there any law

To make a queen say why some spots of red
Lie on her coverlet? or will you say:
Your hands are white, lady, as when you wed,

Where did you bleed? and must I stammer out, Nay,
I blush indeed, fair lord, only to rend
My sleeve up to my shoulder, where there lay

A knife-point last night: so must I defend
The honour of the Lady Guenevere?

Not so, fair lords, even if the world should end

This very day, and you were judges here
Instead of God. Did you see Mellyagraunce
When Launcelot stood by him? what white fear

Curdled his blood, and how his teeth did dance,
His side sink in? as my knight cried and said:
Slayer of unarm'd men, here is a chance!

Setter of traps, I pray you guard your head,
By God I am so glad to fight with you,
Stripper of ladies, that my hand feels lead

For driving weight; hurrah now! draw and do,
For all my wounds are moving in my breast,
And I am getting mad with waiting so.

He struck his hands together o'er the beast,
Who fell down flat, and grovell'd at his feet,
And groan'd at being slain so young: At least,

My knight said, rise you, sir, who are so fleet
At catching ladies, half-arm'd will I fight,
My left side all uncovered! then I weet,

Up sprang Sir Mellyagraunce with great delight
Upon his knave's face; not until just then
Did I quite hate him, as I saw my knight

Along the lists look to my stake and pen
With such a joyous smile, it made me sigh
From agony beneath my waist-chain, when

The fight began, and to me they drew nigh;
Ever Sir Launcelot kept him on the right,
And traversed warily, and ever high

And fast leapt caitiff's sword, until my knight
Sudden threw up his sword to his left hand,
Caught it, and swung it; that was all the fight,

Except a spout of blood on the hot land;
For it was hottest summer; and I know
I wonder'd how the fire, while I should stand,

And burn, against the heat, would quiver so,
Yards above my head; thus these matters went;
Which things were only warnings of the woe

That fell on me. Yet Mellyagraunce was shent,
For Mellyagraunce had fought against the Lord;
Therefore, my lords, take heed lest you be blent

With all this wickedness; say no rash word
Against me, being so beautiful; my eyes,
Wept all away to grey, may bring some sword

To drown you in your blood; see my breast rise,
Like waves of purple sea, as here I stand;
And how my arms are moved in wonderful wise,

Yea also at my full heart's strong command,
See through my long throat how the words go up
In ripples to my mouth; how in my hand

The shadow lies like wine within a cup
Of marvellously colour'd gold; yea now
This little wind is rising, look you up,

And wonder how the light is falling so
Within my moving tresses: will you dare,
When you have looked a little on my brow,

To say this thing is vile? or will you care
For any plausible lies of cunning woof,
When you can see my face with no lie there

For ever? am I not a gracious proof:
But in your chamber Launcelot was found:
Is there a good knight then would stand aloof,

When a queen says with gentle queenly sound:
O true as steel come now and talk with me,

I love to see your step upon the ground

Unwavering, also well I love to see
That gracious smile light up your face, and hear
Your wonderful words, that all mean verily

The thing they seem to mean: good friend, so dear
To me in everything, come here to-night,
Or else the hours will pass most dull and drear;

If you come not, I fear this time I might
Get thinking over much of times gone by,
When I was young, and green hope was in sight:

For no man cares now to know why I sigh;
And no man comes to sing me pleasant songs,
Nor any brings me the sweet flowers that lie

So thick in the gardens; therefore one so longs
To see you, Launcelot; that we may be
Like children once again, free from all wrongs

Just for one night. Did he not come to me?
What thing could keep true Launcelot away
If I said, Come? there was one less than three

In my quiet room that night, and we were gay;
Till sudden I rose up, weak, pale, and sick,
Because a bawling broke our dream up, yea

I looked at Launcelot's face and could not speak,
For he looked helpless too, for a little while;
Then I remember how I tried to shriek,

And could not, but fell down; from tile to tile
The stones they threw up rattled o'er my head
And made me dizzier; till within a while

My maids were all about me, and my head
On Launcelot's breast was being soothed away
From its white chattering, until Launcelot said:

By God! I will not tell you more to-day,
Judge any way you will: what matters it?
You know quite well the story of that fray,

How Launcelot still'd their bawling, the mad fit
That caught up Gauwaine: all, all, verily,
But just that which would save me; these things flit.

Nevertheless you, O Sir Gauwaine, lie,
Whatever may have happen'd these long years,
God knows I speak truth, saying that you lie!

All I have said is truth, by Christ's dear tears.
She would not speak another word, but stood
Turn'd sideways; listening, like a man who hears

His brother's trumpet sounding through the wood
Of his foes' lances. She lean'd eagerly,
And gave a slight spring sometimes, as she could

At last hear something really; joyfully
Her cheek grew crimson, as the headlong speed
Of the roan charger drew all men to see,
The knight who came was Launcelot at good need.

King Arthur's Tomb

Hot August noon: already on that day
   Since sunrise through the Wiltshire downs, most sad
Of mouth and eye, he had gone leagues of way;
   Ay and by night, till whether good or bad

He was, he knew not, though he knew perchance
   That he was Launcelot, the bravest knight
Of all who since the world was, have borne lance,
   Or swung their swords in wrong cause or in right.

Nay, he knew nothing now, except that where
   The Glastonbury gilded towers shine,
A lady dwelt, whose name was Guenevere;
   This he knew also; that some fingers twine,

Not only in a man's hair, even his heart,
   (Making him good or bad I mean,) but in his life,
Skies, earth, men's looks and deeds, all that has part,
   Not being ourselves, in that half-sleep, half-strife,

(Strange sleep, strange strife,) that men call living; so
   Was Launcelot most glad when the moon rose,
Because it brought new memories of her. "Lo,
   Between the trees a large moon, the wind lows

Not loud, but as a cow begins to low,
   Wishing for strength to make the herdsman hear:
The ripe corn gathereth dew; yea, long ago,
   In the old garden life, my Guenevere

Loved to sit still among the flowers, till night
   Had quite come on, hair loosen'd, for she said,
Smiling like heaven, that its fairness might

Draw up the wind sooner to cool her head.

Now while I ride how quick the moon gets small,
    As it did then: I tell myself a tale
That will not last beyond the whitewashed wall,
    Thoughts of some joust must help me through the vale,

Keep this till after: How Sir Gareth ran
    A good course that day under my Queen's eyes,
And how she sway'd laughing at Dinadan.
    No. Back again, the other thoughts will rise,

And yet I think so fast 'twill end right soon:
    Verily then I think, that Guenevere,
Made sad by dew and wind, and tree-barred moon,
    Did love me more than ever, was more dear

To me than ever, she would let me lie
    And kiss her feet, or, if I sat behind,
Would drop her hand and arm most tenderly,
    And touch my mouth. And she would let me wind

Her hair around my neck, so that it fell
    Upon my red robe, strange in the twilight
With many unnamed colours, till the bell
    Of her mouth on my cheek sent a delight

Through all my ways of being; like the stroke
    Wherewith God threw all men upon the face
When he took Enoch, and when Enoch woke
    With a changed body in the happy place.

Once, I remember, as I sat beside,
    She turn'd a little, and laid back her head,
And slept upon my breast; I almost died
    In those night-watches with my love and dread.

There lily-like she bow'd her head and slept,
    And I breathed low, and did not dare to move,
But sat and quiver'd inwardly, thoughts crept,
    And frighten'd me with pulses of my Love.

The stars shone out above the doubtful green
  Of her bodice, in the green sky overhead;
Pale in the green sky were the stars I ween,
  Because the moon shone like a star she shed

When she dwelt up in heaven a while ago,
  And ruled all things but God: the night went on,
The wind grew cold, and the white moon grew low,
  One hand had fallen down, and now lay on

My cold stiff palm; there were no colours then
  For near an hour, and I fell asleep
In spite of all my striving, even when
  I held her whose name-letters make me leap.

I did not sleep long, feeling that in sleep
  I did some loved one wrong, so that the sun
Had only just arisen from the deep
  Still land of colours, when before me one

Stood whom I knew, but scarcely dared to touch,
  She seemed to have changed so in the night;
Moreover she held scarlet lilies, such
  As Maiden Margaret bears upon the light

Of the great church walls, natheless did I walk
  Through the fresh wet woods, and the wheat that morn,
Touching her hair and hand and mouth, and talk
  Of love we held, nigh hid among the corn.

Back to the palace, ere the sun grew high,
  We went, and in a cool green room all day
I gazed upon the arras giddily,
  Where the wind set the silken kings a-sway.

I could not hold her hand, or see her face;
  For which may God forgive me! but I think,
Howsoever, that she was not in that place.
  These memories Launcelot was quick to drink;

And when these fell, some paces past the wall,
  There rose yet others, but they wearied more,

And tasted not so sweet; they did not fall
  So soon, but vaguely wrenched his strained heart sore

In shadowy slipping from his grasp: these gone,
  A longing followed; if he might but touch
That Guenevere at once! Still night, the lone
  Grey horse's head before him vex'd him much,

In steady nodding over the grey road:
  Still night, and night, and night, and emptied heart
Of any stories; what a dismal load
  Time grew at last, yea, when the night did part,

And let the sun flame over all, still there
  The horse's grey ears turn'd this way and that,
And still he watch'd them twitching in the glare
  Of the morning sun, behind them still he sat,

Quite wearied out with all the wretched night,
  Until about the dustiest of the day,
On the last down's brow he drew his rein in sight
  Of the Glastonbury roofs that choke the way.

And he was now quite giddy as before,
  When she slept by him, tired out, and her hair
Was mingled with the rushes on the floor,
  And he, being tired too, was scarce aware

Of her presence; yet as he sat and gazed,
  A shiver ran throughout him, and his breath
Came slower, he seem'd suddenly amazed,
  As though he had not heard of Arthur's death.

This for a moment only, presently
  He rode on giddy still, until he reach'd
A place of apple-trees, by the thorn-tree
  Wherefrom St. Joseph in the days past preached.

Dazed there he laid his head upon a tomb,
  Not knowing it was Arthur's, at which sight
One of her maidens told her, 'He is come,'
  And she went forth to meet him; yet a blight

Had settled on her, all her robes were black,
  With a long white veil only; she went slow,
As one walks to be slain, her eyes did lack
  Half her old glory, yea, alas! the glow

Had left her face and hands; this was because
  As she lay last night on her purple bed,
Wishing for morning, grudging every pause
  Of the palace clocks, until that Launcelot's head

Should lie on her breast, with all her golden hair
  Each side: when suddenly the thing grew drear,
In morning twilight, when the grey downs bare
  Grew into lumps of sin to Guenevere.

At first she said no word, but lay quite still,
  Only her mouth was open, and her eyes
Gazed wretchedly about from hill to hill;
  As though she asked, not with so much surprise

As tired disgust, what made them stand up there
  So cold and grey. After, a spasm took
Her face, and all her frame, she caught her hair,
  All her hair, in both hands, terribly she shook,

And rose till she was sitting in the bed,
  Set her teeth hard, and shut her eyes and seem'd
As though she would have torn it from her head,
  Natheless she dropp'd it, lay down, as she deem'd

It matter'd not whatever she might do:
  O Lord Christ! pity on her ghastly face!
Those dismal hours while the cloudless blue
  Drew the sun higher: He did give her grace;

Because at last she rose up from her bed,
  And put her raiment on, and knelt before
The blessed rood, and with her dry lips said,
  Muttering the words against the marble floor:

'Unless you pardon, what shall I do, Lord,

But go to hell? and there see day by day
Foul deed on deed, hear foulest word on word,
    For ever and ever, such as on the way

To Camelot I heard once from a churl,
    That curled me up upon my jennet's neck
With bitter shame; how then, Lord, should I curl
    For ages and for ages? dost thou reck

That I am beautiful, Lord, even as you
    And your dear mother? why did I forget
You were so beautiful, and good, and true,
    That you loved me so, Guenevere? O yet

If even I go to hell, I cannot choose
    But love you, Christ, yea, though I cannot keep
From loving Launcelot; O Christ! must I lose
    My own heart's love? see, though I cannot weep,

Yet am I very sorry for my sin;
    Moreover, Christ, I cannot bear that hell,
I am most fain to love you, and to win
    A place in heaven some time: I cannot tell:

Speak to me, Christ! I kiss, kiss, kiss your feet;
    Ah! now I weep!' The maid said, 'By the tomb
He waiteth for you, lady,' coming fleet,
    Not knowing what woe filled up all the room.

So Guenevere rose and went to meet him there,
    He did not hear her coming, as he lay
On Arthur's head, till some of her long hair
    Brush'd on the new-cut stone: 'Well done! to pray

For Arthur, my dear Lord, the greatest king
    That ever lived.' 'Guenevere! Guenevere!
Do you not know me, are you gone mad? fling
    Your arms and hair about me, lest I fear

You are not Guenevere, but some other thing.'
    'Pray you forgive me, fair lord Launcelot!
I am not mad, but I am sick; they cling,

God's curses, unto such as I am; not

Ever again shall we twine arms and lips.'
   'Yea, she is mad: thy heavy law, O Lord,
Is very tight about her now, and grips
   Her poor heart, so that no right word

Can reach her mouth; so, Lord, forgive her now,
   That she not knowing what she does, being mad,
Kills me in this way; Guenevere, bend low
   And kiss me once! for God's love kiss me! sad

Though your face is, you look much kinder now;
   Yea once, once for the last time kiss me, lest I die.'
'Christ! my hot lips are very near his brow,
   Help me to save his soul! Yea, verily,

Across my husband's head, fair Launcelot!
   Fair serpent mark'd with V upon the head!
This thing we did while yet he was alive,
   Why not, O twisting knight, now he is dead?

Yea, shake! shake now and shiver! if you can
   Remember anything for agony,
Pray you remember how when the wind ran
   One cool spring evening through fair aspen-tree,

And elm and oak about the palace there,
   The king came back from battle, and I stood
To meet him, with my ladies, on the stair,
   My face made beautiful with my young blood.'

'Will she lie now, Lord God?' 'Remember too,
   Wrung heart, how first before the knights there came
A royal bier, hung round with green and blue,
   About it shone great tapers with sick flame.

And thereupon Lucius, the Emperor,
   Lay royal-robed, but stone-cold now and dead,
Not able to hold sword or sceptre more,
   But not quite grim; because his cloven head

Bore no marks now of Launcelot's bitter sword,
    Being by embalmers deftly solder'd up;
So still it seem'd the face of a great lord,
    Being mended as a craftsman mends a cup.

Also the heralds sung rejoicingly
    To their long trumpets; Fallen under shield,
Here lieth Lucius, King of Italy,
    Slain by Lord Launcelot in open field.

Thereat the people shouted: Launcelot!
    And through the spears I saw you drawing nigh,
You and Lord Arthur: nay, I saw you not,
    But rather Arthur, God would not let die,

I hoped, these many years; he should grow great,
    And in his great arms still encircle me,
Kissing my face, half blinded with the heat
    Of king's love for the queen I used to be.

Launcelot, Launcelot, why did he take your hand,
    When he had kissed me in his kingly way?
Saying: This is the knight whom all the land
    Calls Arthur's banner, sword, and shield to-day;

Cherish him, love. Why did your long lips cleave
    In such strange way unto my fingers then?
So eagerly glad to kiss, so loath to leave
    When you rose up? Why among helmed men

Could I always tell you by your long strong arms,
    And sway like an angel's in your saddle there?
Why sicken'd I so often with alarms
    Over the tilt-yard? Why were you more fair

Than aspens in the autumn at their best?
    Why did you fill all lands with your great fame,
So that Breuse even, as he rode, fear'd lest
    At turning of the way your shield should flame?

Was it nought then, my agony and strife?
    When as day passed by day, year after year,

I found I could not live a righteous life!
   Didst ever think queens held their truth for dear?

O, but your lips say: Yea, but she was cold
   Sometimes, always uncertain as the spring;
When I was sad she would be overbold,
   Longing for kisses. When war-bells did ring,

The back-toll'd bells of noisy Camelot.
   'Now, Lord God, listen! listen, Guenevere,
Though I am weak just now, I think there's not
   A man who dares to say: You hated her,

And left her moaning while you fought your fill
   In the daisied meadows! lo you her thin hand,
That on the carven stone can not keep still,
   Because she loves me against God's command,

Has often been quite wet with tear on tear,
   Tears Launcelot keeps somewhere, surely not
In his own heart, perhaps in Heaven, where
   He will not be these ages.' 'Launcelot!

Loud lips, wrung heart! I say when the bells rang,
   The noisy back-toll'd bells of Camelot,
There were two spots on earth, the thrushes sang
   In the lonely gardens where my love was not,

Where I was almost weeping; I dared not
   Weep quite in those days, lest one maid should say,
In tittering whispers: Where is Launcelot
   To wipe with some kerchief those tears away?

Another answer sharply with brows knit,
   And warning hand up, scarcely lower though:
You speak too loud, see you, she heareth it,
   This tigress fair has claws, as I well know,

As Launcelot knows too, the poor knight! well-a-day!
   Why met he not with Iseult from the West,
Or better still, Iseult of Brittany?
   Perchance indeed quite ladyless were best.

Alas, my maids, you loved not overmuch
  Queen Guenevere, uncertain as sunshine
In March; forgive me! for my sin being such,
  About my whole life, all my deeds did twine,

Made me quite wicked; as I found out then,
  I think; in the lonely palace where each morn
We went, my maids and I, to say prayers when
  They sang mass in the chapel on the lawn.

And every morn I scarce could pray at all,
  For Launcelot's red-golden hair would play,
Instead of sunlight, on the painted wall,
  Mingled with dreams of what the priest did say;

Grim curses out of Peter and of Paul;
  Judging of strange sins in Leviticus;
Another sort of writing on the wall,
  Scored deep across the painted heads of us.

Christ sitting with the woman at the well,
  And Mary Magdalen repenting there,
Her dimmed eyes scorch'd and red at sight of hell
  So hardly 'scaped, no gold light on her hair.

And if the priest said anything that seemed
  To touch upon the sin they said we did,
(This in their teeth) they looked as if they deem'd
  That I was spying what thoughts might be hid

Under green-cover'd bosoms, heaving quick
  Beneath quick thoughts; while they grew red with shame,
And gazed down at their feet: while I felt sick,
  And almost shriek'd if one should call my name.

The thrushes sang in the lone garden there:
  But where you were the birds were scared I trow:
Clanging of arms about pavilions fair,
  Mixed with the knights' laughs; there, as I well know,

Rode Launcelot, the king of all the band,

And scowling Gauwaine, like the night in day,
  And handsome Gareth, with his great white hand
    Curl'd round the helm-crest, ere he join'd the fray;

And merry Dinadan with sharp dark face,
  All true knights loved to see; and in the fight
Great Tristram, and though helmed you could trace
  In all his bearing the frank noble knight;

And by him Palomydes, helmet off,
  He fought, his face brush'd by his hair,
Red heavy swinging hair; he fear'd a scoff
  So overmuch, though what true knight would dare

To mock that face, fretted with useless care,
  And bitter useless striving after love?
O Palomydes, with much honour bear
  Beast Glatysaunt upon your shield, above

Your helm that hides the swinging of your hair,
  And think of Iseult, as your sword drives through
Much mail and plate: O God, let me be there
  A little time, as I was long ago!

Because stout Gareth lets his spear fall low,
  Gauwaine and Launcelot, and Dinadan
Are helm'd and waiting; let the trumpets go!
  Bend over, ladies, to see all you can!

Clench teeth, dames, yea, clasp hands, for Gareth's spear
  Throws Kay from out his saddle, like a stone
From a castle-window when the foe draws near:
  Iseult! Sir Dinadan rolleth overthrown.

Iseult! again: the pieces of each spear
  Fly fathoms up, and both the great steeds reel;
Tristram for Iseult! Iseult! and Guenevere!
  The ladies' names bite verily like steel.

They bite: bite me, Lord God! I shall go mad,
  Or else die kissing him, he is so pale,
He thinks me mad already, O bad! bad!

Let me lie down a little while and wail.'

'No longer so, rise up, I pray you, love,
    And slay me really, then we shall be heal'd,
Perchance, in the aftertime by God above.'
    'Banner of Arthur, with black-bended shield

Sinister-wise across the fair gold ground!
    Here let me tell you what a knight you are,
O sword and shield of Arthur! you are found
    A crooked sword, I think, that leaves a scar

On the bearer's arm, so be he thinks it straight,
    Twisted Malay's crease beautiful blue-grey,
Poison'd with sweet fruit; as he found too late,
    My husband Arthur, on some bitter day!

O sickle cutting hemlock the day long!
    That the husbandman across his shoulder hangs,
And, going homeward about evensong,
    Dies the next morning, struck through by the fangs!

Banner, and sword, and shield, you dare not die,
    Lest you meet Arthur in the other world,
And, knowing who you are, he pass you by,
    Taking short turns that he may watch you curl'd,

Body and face and limbs in agony,
    Lest he weep presently and go away,
Saying: I loved him once, with a sad sigh,
    Now I have slain him, Lord, let me go too, I pray.

                                        [Launcelot *falls.*

Alas! alas! I know not what to do,
    If I run fast it is perchance that I
May fall and stun myself, much better so,
    Never, never again! not even when I die.'

LAUNCELOT,
on awaking.
'I stretch'd my hands towards her and fell down,
    How long I lay in swoon I cannot tell:

My head and hands were bleeding from the stone,
  When I rose up, also I heard a bell.'

Sir Galahad, A Christmas Mystery

It is the longest night in all the year,
   Near on the day when the Lord Christ was born;
Six hours ago I came and sat down here,
   And ponder'd sadly, wearied and forlorn.

The winter wind that pass'd the chapel door,
   Sang out a moody tune, that went right well
With mine own thoughts: I look'd down on the floor,
   Between my feet, until I heard a bell

Sound a long way off through the forest deep,
   And toll on steadily; a drowsiness
Came on me, so that I fell half asleep,
   As I sat there not moving: less and less

I saw the melted snow that hung in beads
   Upon my steel-shoes; less and less I saw
Between the tiles the bunches of small weeds:
   Heartless and stupid, with no touch of awe

Upon me, half-shut eyes upon the ground,
   I thought: O Galahad! the days go by,
Stop and cast up now that which you have found,
   So sorely you have wrought and painfully.

Night after night your horse treads down alone
   The sere damp fern, night after night you sit
Holding the bridle like a man of stone,
   Dismal, unfriended: what thing comes of it?

And what if Palomydes also ride,

And over many a mountain and bare heath
Follow the questing beast with none beside?
  Is he not able still to hold his breath

With thoughts of Iseult? doth he not grow pale
  With weary striving, to seem best of all
To her, 'as she is best,' he saith? to fail
  Is nothing to him, he can never fall.

For unto such a man love-sorrow is
  So dear a thing unto his constant heart,
That even if he never win one kiss,
  Or touch from Iseult, it will never part.

And he will never know her to be worse
  Than in his happiest dreams he thinks she is:
Good knight, and faithful, you have 'scaped the curse
  In wonderful-wise; you have great store of bliss.

Yea, what if Father Launcelot ride out,
  Can he not think of Guenevere's arms, round
Warm and lithe, about his neck, and shout
  Till all the place grows joyful with the sound?

And when he lists can often see her face,
  And think, 'Next month I kiss you, or next week,
And still you think of me': therefore the place
  Grows very pleasant, whatsoever he seek.

But me, who ride alone, some carle shall find
  Dead in my arms in the half-melted snow,
When all unkindly with the shifting wind,
  The thaw comes on at Candlemas: I know

Indeed that they will say: 'This Galahad
  If he had lived had been a right good knight;
Ah! poor chaste body!' but they will be glad,
  Not most alone, but all, when in their sight

That very evening in their scarlet sleeves
  The gay-dress'd minstrels sing; no maid will talk
Of sitting on my tomb, until the leaves,

Grown big upon the bushes of the walk,

East of the Palace-pleasaunce, make it hard
   To see the minster therefrom: well-a-day!
Before the trees by autumn were well bared,
   I saw a damozel with gentle play,

Within that very walk say last farewell
   To her dear knight, just riding out to find
(Why should I choke to say it?) the Sangreal,
   And their last kisses sunk into my mind,

Yea, for she stood lean'd forward on his breast,
   Rather, scarce stood; the back of one dear hand,
That it might well be kiss'd, she held and press'd
   Against his lips; long time they stood there, fann'd

By gentle gusts of quiet frosty wind,
   Till Mador de la porte a-going by,
And my own horsehoofs roused them; they untwined,
   And parted like a dream. In this way I,

With sleepy face bent to the chapel floor,
   Kept musing half asleep, till suddenly
A sharp bell rang from close beside the door,
   And I leapt up when something pass'd me by,

Shrill ringing going with it, still half blind
   I stagger'd after, a great sense of awe
At every step kept gathering on my mind,
   Thereat I have no marvel, for I saw

One sitting on the altar as a throne,
   Whose face no man could say he did not know,
And though the bell still rang, he sat alone,
   With raiment half blood-red, half white as snow.

Right so I fell upon the floor and knelt,
   Not as one kneels in church when mass is said,
But in a heap, quite nerveless, for I felt
   The first time what a thing was perfect dread.

But mightily the gentle voice came down:
   'Rise up, and look and listen, Galahad,
Good knight of God, for you will see no frown
   Upon my face; I come to make you glad.

For that you say that you are all alone,
   I will be with you always, and fear not
You are uncared for, though no maiden moan
   Above your empty tomb; for Launcelot,

He in good time shall be my servant too,
   Meantime, take note whose sword first made him knight,
And who has loved him alway, yea, and who
   Still trusts him alway, though in all men's sight,

He is just what you know, O Galahad,
   This love is happy even as you say,
But would you for a little time be glad,
   To make *me* sorry long, day after day?

Her warm arms round his neck half throttle *me*,
   The hot love-tears burn deep like spots of lead,
Yea, and the years pass quick: right dismally
   Will Launcelot at one time hang his head;

Yea, old and shrivell'd he shall win my love.
   Poor Palomydes fretting out his soul!
Not always is he able, son, to move
   His love, and do it honour: needs must roll

The proudest destrier sometimes in the dust,
   And then 'tis weary work; he strives beside
Seem better than he is, so that his trust
   Is always on what chances may betide;

And so he wears away, my servant, too,
   When all these things are gone, and wretchedly
He sits and longs to moan for Iseult, who
   Is no care now to Palomydes: see,

O good son Galahad, upon this day,
   Now even, all these things are on your side,

But these you fight not for; look up, I say,
    And see how I can love you, for no pride

Closes your eyes, no vain lust keeps them down.
    See now you have *me* always; following
That holy vision, Galahad, go on,
    Until at last you come to *me* to sing

In Heaven always, and to walk around
    The garden where I am.' He ceased, my face
And wretched body fell upon the ground;
    And when I look'd again, the holy place

Was empty; but right so the bell again
    Came to the chapel-door, there entered
Two angels first, in white, without a stain,
    And scarlet wings, then, after them, a bed

Four ladies bore, and set it down beneath
    The very altar-step, and while for fear
I scarcely dared to move or draw my breath,
    Those holy ladies gently came a-near,

And quite unarm'd me, saying: 'Galahad,
    Rest here awhile and sleep, and take no thought
Of any other thing than being glad;
    Hither the Sangreal will be shortly brought,

Yet must you sleep the while it stayeth here.'
    Right so they went away, and I, being weary,
Slept long and dream'd of Heaven: the bell comes near,
    I doubt it grows to morning. Miserere!
        Enter Two Angels in white, with scarlet wings; also, Four Ladies in gowns
            of red and green; also an Angel, bearing in his hands a surcoat of
            white, with a red cross.

AN ANGEL

O servant of the high God, Galahad!
    Rise and be arm'd: the Sangreal is gone forth
Through the great forest, and you must be had
    Unto the sea that lieth on the north:

There shall you find the wondrous ship wherein
  The spindles of King Solomon are laid,
And the sword that no man draweth without sin,
  But if he be most pure: and there is stay'd,

Hard by, Sir Launcelot, whom you will meet
  In some short space upon that ship: first, though,
Will come here presently that lady sweet,
  Sister of Percival, whom you well know,

And with her Bors and Percival: stand now,
  These ladies will to arm you.

FIRST LADY,
putting on the hauberk.
Galahad,

That I may stand so close beneath your brow,
  I, Margaret of Antioch, am glad.

SECOND LADY,
girding him with the sword.

That I may stand and touch you with my hand,
  O Galahad, I, Cecily, am glad.

THIRD LADY,
buckling on the spurs.

That I may kneel while up above you stand,
  And gaze at me, O holy Galahad,

I, Lucy, am most glad.

FOURTH LADY,
putting on the basnet.
O gentle knight,

That you bow down to us in reverence,
We are most glad, I, Katherine, with delight
  Must needs fall trembling.

ANGEL,
putting on the crossed surcoat.
Galahad, we go hence,

For here, amid the straying of the snow,

Come Percival's sister, Bors, and Percival.

> [*The Four Ladies carry out the bed,*
> *and all go but* Galahad.

GALAHAD

How still and quiet everything seems now:
    They come, too, for I hear the horsehoofs fall.

        Enter Sir Bors, Sir Percival, *and* his Sister.

Fair friends and gentle lady, God you save!
    A many marvels have been here to-night;
Tell me what news of Launcelot you have,
    And has God's body ever been in sight?

SIR BORS

Why, as for seeing that same holy thing,
    As we were riding slowly side by side,
An hour ago, we heard a sweet voice sing,
    And through the bare twigs saw a great light glide,

With many-colour'd raiment, but far off;
    And so pass'd quickly: from the court nought good;
Poor merry Dinadan, that with jape and scoff
    Kept us all merry, in a little wood

Was found all hack'd and dead: Sir Lionel
    And Gauwaine have come back from the great quest,
Just merely shamed; and Lauvaine, who loved well
    Your father Launcelot, at the king's behest

Went out to seek him, but was almost slain,
    Perhaps is dead now; everywhere
The knights come foil'd from the great quest, in vain;
    In vain they struggle for the vision fair.

The Chapel in Lyoness

SIR OZANA LE CURE HARDY. SIR GALAHAD. SIR
BORS DE GANYS.

SIR OZANA

All day long and every day,
From Christmas-Eve to Whit-Sunday,
Within that Chapel-aisle I lay,
   And no man came a-near.

Naked to the waist was I,
And deep within my breast did lie,
Though no man any blood could spy,
   The truncheon of a spear.

No meat did ever pass my lips
Those days. Alas! the sunlight slips
From off the gilded parclose, dips,
   And night comes on apace.

My arms lay back behind my head;
Over my raised-up knees was spread
A samite cloth of white and red;
   A rose lay on my face.

Many a time I tried to shout;
But as in dream of battle-rout,
My frozen speech would not well out;
   I could not even weep.

With inward sigh I see the sun
Fade off the pillars one by one,
My heart faints when the day is done,
   Because I cannot sleep.

Sometimes strange thoughts pass through my head;
Not like a tomb is this my bed,
Yet oft I think that I am dead;
   That round my tomb is writ,

'Ozana of the hardy heart,
   Knight of the Table Round,
Pray for his soul, lords, of your part;
   A true knight he was found.'
Ah! me, I cannot fathom it.

                                  [*He sleeps.*

SIR GALAHAD.

All day long and every day,
Till his madness pass'd away,
I watch'd Ozana as he lay
   Within the gilded screen.

All my singing moved him not;
As I sung my heart grew hot,
With the thought of Launcelot
   Far away, I ween.

So I went a little space
From out the chapel, bathed my face
In the stream that runs apace
   By the churchyard wall.

There I pluck'd a faint wild rose,
Hard by where the linden grows,
Sighing over silver rows
   Of the lilies tall.

I laid the flower across his mouth;
The sparkling drops seem'd good for drouth;
He smiled, turn'd round towards the south.
   Held up a golden tress.

The light smote on it from the west;
He drew the covering from his breast,
Against his heart that hair he prest;

Death him soon will bless.

SIR BORS

I enter'd by the western door;
   I saw a knight's helm lying there:
I raised my eyes from off the floor,
   And caught the gleaming of his hair.

I stept full softly up to him;
   I laid my chin upon his head;
I felt him smile; my eyes did swim,
   I was so glad he was not dead.

I heard Ozana murmur low,
   'There comes no sleep nor any love.'
But Galahad stoop'd and kiss'd his brow:
   He shiver'd; I saw his pale lips move.

SIR OZANA

There comes no sleep nor any love;
   Ah me! I shiver with delight.
I am so weak I cannot move;
   God move me to thee, dear, to-night!
Christ help! I have but little wit:
My life went wrong; I see it writ,

'Ozana of the hardy heart,
   Knight of the Table Round,
Pray for his soul, lords, on your part;
   A good knight he was found.'

Now I begin to fathom it.

                                         [*He dies.*

SIR BORS

Galahad sits dreamily;
What strange things may his eyes see,
Great blue eyes fix'd full on me?
On his soul, Lord, have mercy.

SIR GALAHAD

Ozana, shall I pray for thee?
Her cheek is laid to thine;
No long time hence, also I see
  Thy wasted fingers twine

Within the tresses of her hair
  That shineth gloriously,
Thinly outspread in the clear air
  Against the jasper sea.

Sir Peter Harpdon's End

In an English Castle in Poictou.
Sir Peter Harpdon, *a Gascon knight in the English service, and* John
  Curzon, *his lieutenant.*

JOHN CURZON.

Of those three prisoners, that before you came
We took down at St. John's hard by the mill,
Two are good masons; we have tools enough,
And you have skill to set them working.

SIR PETER.
So:

What are their names?

JOHN CURZON.
Why, Jacques Aquadent,
And Peter Plombiere, but,

SIR PETER.
What colour'd hair
Has Peter now? has Jacques got bow legs?

JOHN CURZON.
Why, sir, you jest: what matters Jacques' hair,
Or Peter's legs to us?

SIR PETER.
O! John, John, John!
Throw all your mason's tools down the deep well,
Hang Peter up and Jacques; They're no good,
We shall not build, man.

JOHN CURZON

(going).

Shall I call the guard
To hang them, sir? and yet, sir, for the tools,
We'd better keep them still; sir, fare you well.

[Muttering as he goes.

What have I done that he should jape at me?
And why not build? the walls are weak enough,
And we've two masons and a heap of tools.

[Goes, still muttering.

SIR PETER.

To think a man should have a lump like that
For his lieutenant! I must call him back,
Or else, as surely as St. George is dead,
He'll hang our friends the masons: here, John! John!

JOHN CURZON.

At your good service, sir.

SIR PETER.

Come now, and talk
This weighty matter out; there, we've no stone
To mend our walls with, neither brick nor stone.

JOHN CURZON.

There is a quarry, sir, some ten miles off.

SIR PETER.

We are not strong enough to send ten men
Ten miles to fetch us stone enough to build.
In three hours' time they would be taken or slain,
The cursed Frenchmen ride abroad so thick.

JOHN CURZON.

But we can send some villaynes to get stone.

SIR PETER.

Alas! John, that we cannot bring them back,
They would go off to Clisson or Sanxere,
And tell them we were weak in walls and men,

Then down go we; for, look you, times are changed,
And now no longer does the country shake
At sound of English names; our captains fade
From off our muster-rolls. At Lusac bridge
I daresay you may even yet see the hole
That Chandos beat in dying; far in Spain
Pembroke is prisoner; Phelton prisoner here;
Manny lies buried in the Charterhouse;
Oliver Clisson turn'd these years agone;
The Captal died in prison; and, over all,
Edward the prince lies underneath the ground,
Edward the king is dead, at Westminster
The carvers smooth the curls of his long beard.
Everything goes to rack — eh! and we too.
Now, Curzon, listen; if they come, these French,
Whom have I got to lean on here, but you?
A man can die but once, will you die then,
Your brave sword in your hand, thoughts in your heart
Of all the deeds we have done here in France —
And yet may do? So God will have your soul,
Whoever has your body.

JOHN CURZON.
Why, sir, I
Will fight till the last moment, until then
Will do whate'er you tell me. Now I see
We must e'en leave the walls; well, well, perhaps
They're stronger than I think for; pity, though!
For some few tons of stone, if Guesclin comes.

SIR PETER.
Farewell, John, pray you watch the Gascons well,
I doubt them.

JOHN CURZON.
Truly, sir, I will watch well.

[Goes.

SIR PETER.
Farewell, good lump! and yet, when all is said,
'Tis a good lump. Why then, if Guesclin comes;
Some dozen stones from his petrariae,

And, under shelter of his crossbows, just
An hour's steady work with pickaxes,
Then a great noise — some dozen swords and glaives
A-playing on my basnet all at once,
And little more cross purposes on earth
For me.

         Now this is hard: a month ago,
And a few minutes' talk had set things right
'Twixt me and Alice; if she had a doubt,
As, may Heaven bless her! I scarce think she had,
'Twas but their hammer, hammer in her ears,
Of how Sir Peter fail'd at Lusac Bridge:
And how he was grown moody of late days;
And how Sir Lambert, think now! his dear friend,
His sweet, dear cousin, could not but confess
That Peter's talk tended towards the French,
Which he, for instance Lambert, was glad of,
Being, Lambert, you see, on the French side.

                               Well,

If I could but have seen her on that day,
Then, when they sent me off!

                    I like to think,
Although it hurts me, makes my head twist, what,
If I had seen her, what I should have said,
What she, my darling, would have said and done.
As thus perchance.

             To find her sitting there,
In the window-seat, not looking well at all,
Crying perhaps, and I say quietly:
Alice! she looks up, chokes a sob, looks grave,
Changes from pale to red, but, ere she speaks,
Straightway I kneel down there on both my knees,
And say: O lady, have I sinn'd, your knight?
That still you ever let me walk alone
In the rose garden, that you sing no songs
When I am by, that ever in the dance
You quietly walk away when I come near?
Now that I have you, will you go, think you?

  Ere she could answer I would speak again,
Still kneeling there.

             What! they have frighted you,

By hanging burs, and clumsily carven puppets,
Round my good name; but afterwards, my love,
I will say what this means; this moment, see!
Do I kneel here, and can you doubt me? Yea:
For she would put her hands upon my face:
Yea, that is best, yea feel, love, am I changed?
And she would say: Good knight, come, kiss my lips!
And afterwards as I sat there would say:

Please a poor silly girl by telling me
What all those things they talk of really were,
For it is true you did not help Chandos,
And true, poor love! you could not come to me
When I was in such peril.
                              I should say:
I am like Balen, all things turn to blame.
I did not come to you? At Bergerath
The constable had held us close shut up,
If from the barriers I had made three steps,
I should have been but slain; at Lusac, too,
We struggled in a marish half the day,
And came too late at last: you know, my love,
How heavy men and horses are all arm'd.
All that Sir Lambert said was pure, unmix'd,
Quite groundless lies; as you can think, sweet love.

She, holding tight my hand as we sat there,
Started a little at Sir Lambert's name,
But otherwise she listen'd scarce at all
To what I said. Then with moist, weeping eyes,
And quivering lips, that scarcely let her speak,
She said: I love you.
                         Other words were few,
The remnant of that hour; her hand smooth'd down
My foolish head; she kiss'd me all about
My face, and through the tangles of my beard
Her little fingers crept!

                         O God, my Alice,
Not this good way: my lord but sent and said
That Lambert's sayings were taken at their worth,
Therefore that day I was to start, and keep

This hold against the French; and I am here:

                                          [Looks out of the window.

A sprawling lonely garde with rotten walls,
And no one to bring aid if Guesclin comes,
Or any other.

                       There's a pennon now!
At last.

                 But not the constable's: whose arms,
I wonder, does it bear? Three golden rings
On a red ground; my cousin's by the rood!
Well, I should like to kill him, certainly,
But to be kill'd by him:

                                      [A trumpet sounds.

                      That's for a herald;
I doubt this does not mean assaulting yet.

        Enter John Curzon.

What says the herald of our cousin, sir?

JOHN CURZON.

So please you, sir, concerning your estate,
He has good will to talk with you.

SIR PETER.
                         Outside,

I'll talk with him, close by the gate St. Ives.
Is he unarm'd?

JOHN CURZON.
Yea, sir, in a long gown.

SIR PETER.
Then bid them bring me hither my furr'd gown
With the long sleeves, and under it I'll wear,
By Lambert's leave, a secret coat of mail;
And will you lend me, John, your little axe?
I mean the one with Paul wrought on the blade?
And I will carry it inside my sleeve,
Good to be ready always; you, John, go
And bid them set up many suits of arms,
Bows, archgays, lances, in the base-court, and

Yourself, from the south postern setting out,
With twenty men, be ready to break through
Their unguarded rear when I cry out, St. George!

JOHN CURZON.

How, sir! will you attack him unawares,
And slay him unarm'd?

SIR PETER.
Trust me, John, I know

The reason why he comes here with sleeved gown,
Fit to hide axes up. So, let us go.

[They go.

Outside the castle by the great gate; Sir Lambert and Sir Peter seated;
guards attending each, the rest of Sir Lambert's men drawn up
about a furlong off.

SIR PETER.

And if I choose to take the losing side
Still, does it hurt you?

SIR LAMBERT
O! no hurt to me;

I see you sneering, Why take trouble then,
Seeing you love me not? Look you, our house
(Which, taken altogether, I love much)
Had better be upon the right side now,
If, once for all, it wishes to bear rule
As such a house should: cousin, you're too wise
To feed your hope up fat, that this fair France
Will ever draw two ways again; this side
The French, wrong-headed, all a-jar
With envious longings; and the other side
The order'd English, orderly led on
By those two Edwards through all wrong and right,
And muddling right and wrong to a thick broth
With that long stick, their strength. This is all changed,
The true French win, on either side you have
Cool-headed men, good at a tilting match,
And good at setting battles in array,
And good at squeezing taxes at due time;

Therefore by nature we French being here
Upon our own big land:

                              [*Sir Peter laughs aloud.*

                    Well, Peter! well!
What makes you laugh?

SIR PETER.
                    Hearing you sweat to prove
All this I know so well; but you have read
The siege of Troy?

SIR LAMBERT.
                    O! yea, I know it well.

SIR PETER.
There! they were wrong, as wrong as men could be
For, as I think, they found it such delight
To see fair Helen going through their town;
Yea, any little common thing she did
(As stooping to pick a flower) seem'd so strange,
So new in its great beauty, that they said:
Here we will keep her living in this town,
Till all burns up together. And so, fought,
In a mad whirl of knowing they were wrong;
Yea, they fought well, and ever, like a man
That hangs legs off the ground by both his hands,
Over some great height, did they struggle sore,
Quite sure to slip at last; wherefore, take note
How almost all men, reading that sad siege,
Hold for the Trojans; as I did at least,
Thought Hector the best knight a long way:

                              Now

Why should I not do this thing that I think;
For even when I come to count the gains,
I have them my side: men will talk, you know
(We talk of Hector, dead so long agone,)
When I am dead, of how this Peter clung
To what he thought the right; of how he died,
Perchance, at last, doing some desperate deed
Few men would care do now, and this is gain
To me, as ease and money is to you.
Moreover, too, I like the straining game

Of striving well to hold up things that fall;
So one becomes great. See you! in good times
All men live well together, and you, too,
Live dull and happy: happy? not so quick,
Suppose sharp thoughts begin to burn you up?
Why then, but just to fight as I do now,
A halter round my neck, would be great bliss.
O! I am well off.

[Aside.

                 Talk, and talk, and talk,
I know this man has come to murder me,
And yet I talk still.

SIR LAMBERT.
               If your side were right,
You might be, though you lost; but if I said,
'You are a traitor, being, as you are,
Born Frenchman.' What are Edwards unto you,
Or Richards?

SIR PETER.
        Nay, hold there, my Lambert, hold!
For fear your zeal should bring you to some harm,
Don't call me traitor.

SIR LAMBERT.
           Furthermore, my knight,
Men call you slippery on your losing side,
When at Bordeaux I was ambassador,
I heard them say so, and could scarce say: Nay.

[He takes hold of something in
his sleeve, and rises.

SIR PETER,
rising.

They lied: and you lie, not for the first time.
What have you got there, fumbling up your sleeve,
A stolen purse?

SIR LAMBERT.
         Nay, liar in your teeth!
Dead liar too; St. Denis and St. Lambert!

[*Strikes at* Sir Peter *with a dagger.*

SIR PETER,
striking him flatlings with his axe.
How thief! thief! thief! so there, fair thief, so there,
St. George Guienne! glaives for the castellan!
You French, you are but dead, unless you lay
Your spears upon the earth. St. George Guienne!

Well done, John Curzon, how he has them now.

In the Castle.

JOHN CURZON.
What shall we do with all these prisoners, sir?

SIR PETER.
Why, put them all to ransom, those that can
Pay anything, but not too light though, John,
Seeing we have them on the hip: for those
That have no money, that being certified,
Why, turn them out of doors before they spy;
But bring Sir Lambert guarded unto me.

JOHN CURZON.
I will, fair sir.

[*He goes.*

SIR PETER.
I do not wish to kill him,
Although I think I ought; he shall go mark'd,
By all the saints, though!
          Enter Lambert *guarded.*
                    Now, Sir Lambert, now!
What sort of death do you expect to get,
Being taken this way?

SIR LAMBERT.
Cousin! cousin! think!
I am your own blood; may God pardon me!
I am not fit to die; if you knew all,
All I have done since I was young and good.

O! you would give me yet another chance,
As God would, that I might wash all clear out,
By serving you and Him. Let me go now!
And I will pay you down more golden crowns
Of ransom than the king would!

SIR PETER.
                              Well, stand back,
And do not touch me! No, you shall not die,
Nor yet pay ransom. You, John Curzon, cause
Some carpenters to build a scaffold, high,
Outside the gate; when it is built, sound out
To all good folks, 'Come, see a traitor punish'd!'
Take me my knight, and set him up thereon,
And let the hangman shave his head quite clean,
And cut his ears off close up to the head;
And cause the minstrels all the while to play
Soft music, and good singing; for this day
Is my high day of triumph; is it not,
Sir Lambert?

SIR LAMBERT.
              Ah! on your own blood,
Own name, you heap this foul disgrace? you dare,
With hands and fame thus sullied, to go back
And take the lady Alice?

SIR PETER.
                    Say her name
Again, and you are dead, slain here by me.
Why should I talk with you? I'm master here,
And do not want your schooling; is it not
My mercy that you are not dangling dead
There in the gateway with a broken neck?

SIR LAMBERT.
Such mercy! why not kill me then outright?
To die is nothing; but to live that all
May point their fingers! yea, I'd rather die.

JOHN CURZON.
Why, will it make you any uglier man

To lose your ears? they're much too big for you,
You ugly Judas!

SIR PETER.

[*To* Lambert.

That's your choice,
To die, mind! Then you shall die: Lambert mine,
I thank you now for choosing this so well,
It saves me much perplexity and doubt;
Perchance an ill deed too, for half I count
This sparing traitors is an ill deed.

Well,
Lambert, die bravely, and we're almost friends.

SIR LAMBERT,
grovelling.
O God! this is a fiend and not a man;
Will some one save me from him? help, help, help!
I will not die.

SIR PETER.
Why, what is this I see?
A man who is a knight, and bandied words
So well just now with me, is lying down,
Gone mad for fear like this! So, so, you thought
You knew the worst, and might say what you pleased.
I should have guess'd this from a man like you.
Eh! righteous Job would give up skin for skin,
Yea, all a man can have for simple life,
And we talk fine, yea, even a hound like this,
Who needs must know that when he dies, deep hell
Will hold him fast for ever, so fine we talk,
'Would rather die,' all that. Now sir, get up!
And choose again: shall it be head sans ears,
Or trunk sans head?
John Curzon, pull him up!
What, life then? go and build the scaffold, John.
  Lambert, I hope that never on this earth
We meet again; that you'll turn out a monk,
And mend the life I give you, so farewell,
I'm sorry you're a rascal. John, despatch.

In the French camp before the Castle.
Sir Peter *prisoner,* Guesclin, Clisson, Sir Lambert.

SIR PETER.

So now is come the ending of my life;
If I could clear this sickening lump away
That sticks in my dry throat, and say a word,
Guesclin might listen.

GUESCLIN.
                    Tell me, fair sir knight,
If you have been clean liver before God,
And then you need not fear much; as for me,
I cannot say I hate you, yet my oath,
And cousin Lambert's ears here clench the thing.

SIR PETER.

I knew you could not hate me, therefore I
Am bold to pray for life; 'twill harm your cause
To hang knights of good name, harms here in France
I have small doubt, at any rate hereafter
Men will remember you another way
Than I should care to be remember'd, ah!
Although hot lead runs through me for my blood,
All this falls cold as though I said, Sweet lords,
Give back my falcon!
                    See how young I am,
Do you care altogether more for France,
Say rather one French faction, than for all
The state of Christendom? a gallant knight,
As (yea, by God!) I have been, is more worth
Than many castles; will you bring this death,
For a mere act of justice, on my head?

Think how it ends all, death! all other things
Can somehow be retrieved, yea, send me forth
Naked and maimed, rather than slay me here;
Then somehow will I get me other clothes,
And somehow will I get me some poor horse,
And, somehow clad in poor old rusty arms,
Will ride and smite among the serried glaives,

Fear not death so; for I can tilt right well,
Let me not say I could; I know all tricks,
That sway the sharp sword cunningly; ah you,
You, my Lord Clisson, in the other days
Have seen me learning these, yea, call to mind,
How in the trodden corn by Chartres town,
When you were nearly swooning from the back
Of your black horse, those three blades slid at once
From off my sword's edge; pray for me, my lord!

CLISSON.

Nay, this is pitiful, to see him die.
My Lord the Constable, I pray you note
That you are losing some few thousand crowns
By slaying this man; also think: his lands
Along the Garonne river lie for leagues,
And are right rich, a many mills he has,
Three abbeys of grey monks do hold of him:
Though wishing well for Clement, as we do,
I know the next heir, his old uncle, well,
Who does not care two deniers for the knight
As things go now, but slay him, and then see,
How he will bristle up like any perch,
With curves of spears. What! do not doubt, my lord,
You'll get the money, this man saved my life,
And I will buy him for two thousand crowns;
Well, five then: eh! what! No again? well then,
Ten thousand crowns?

GUESCLIN.

My sweet lord, much I grieve
I cannot please you, yea, good sooth, I grieve
This knight must die, as verily he must;
For I have sworn it, so men take him out,
Use him not roughly.

SIR LAMBERT,
coming forward.
Music, do you know,
Music will suit you well, I think, because
You look so mild, like Laurence being grill'd;
Or perhaps music soft and slow, because

This is high day of triumph unto me,
Is it not, Peter?
                    You are frighten'd, though,
Eh! you are pale, because this hurts you much,
Whose life was pleasant to you, not like mine,
You ruin'd wretch! Men mock me in the streets,
Only in whispers loud, because I am
Friend of the constable; will this please you,
Unhappy Peter? once a-going home,
Without my servants, and a little drunk,
At midnight through the lone dim lamp-lit streets.
A whore came up and spat into my eyes,
Rather to blind me than to make me see,
But she was very drunk, and tottering back,
Even in the middle of her laughter fell
And cut her head against the pointed stones,
While I lean'd on my staff, and look'd at her,
And cried, being drunk.
                    Girls would not spit at you.
You are so handsome, I think verily
Most ladies would be glad to kiss your eyes,
And yet you will be hung like a cur dog
Five minutes hence, and grow black in the face,
And curl your toes up. Therefore I am glad.

    Guess why I stand and talk this nonsense now,
With Guesclin getting ready to play chess,
And Clisson doing something with his sword,
I can't see what, talking to Guesclin though,
I don't know what about, perhaps of you.
But, cousin Peter, while I stroke your beard,
Let me say this, I'd like to tell you now
That your life hung upon a game of chess,
That if, say, my squire Robert here should beat,
Why you should live, but hang if I beat him;
Then guess, clever Peter, what I should do then:
Well, give it up? why, Peter, I should let
My squire Robert beat me, then you would think
That you were safe, you know; Eh? not at all,
But I should keep you three days in some hold,
Giving you salt to eat, which would be kind,
Considering the tax there is on salt;

And afterwards should let you go, perhaps?
No I should not, but I should hang you, sir,
With a red rope in lieu of mere grey rope.

But I forgot, you have not told me yet
If you can guess why I talk nonsense thus,
Instead of drinking wine while you are hang'd?
You are not quick at guessing, give it up.
This is the reason; here I hold your hand,
And watch you growing paler, see you writhe
And this, my Peter, is a joy so dear,
I cannot by all striving tell you how
I love it, nor I think, good man, would you
Quite understand my great delight therein;
You, when you had me underneath you once,
Spat as it were, and said, 'Go take him out,'
That they might do that thing to me whereat,
E'en now this long time off I could well shriek,
And then you tried forget I ever lived,
And sunk your hating into other things;
While I: St. Denis! though, I think you'll faint,
Your lips are grey so; yes, you will, unless
You let it out and weep like a hurt child;
Hurrah! you do now. Do not go just yet,
For I am Alice, am right like her now,
Will you not kiss me on the lips, my love?

CLISSON.

You filthy beast, stand back and let him go,
Or by God's eyes I'll choke you!

                              [*Kneeling to* Sir Peter.
                    Fair sir knight
I kneel upon my knees and pray to you
That you would pardon me for this your death;
God knows how much I wish you still alive,
Also how heartily I strove to save
Your life at this time; yea, he knows quite well,
(I swear it, so forgive me!) how I would,
If it were possible, give up my life
Upon this grass for yours; fair knight, although,
He knowing all things knows this thing too, well,
Yet when you see his face some short time hence,

Tell him I tried to save you.

SIR PETER
                    O! my lord,
I cannot say this is as good as life,
But yet it makes me feel far happier now,
And if at all, after a thousand years,
I see God's face, I will speak loud and bold,
And tell Him you were kind, and like Himself;
Sir, may God bless you!
                    Did you note how I
Fell weeping just now? pray you, do not think
That Lambert's taunts did this, I hardly heard
The base things that he said, being deep in thought
Of all things that have happen'd since I was
A little child; and so at last I thought
Of my true lady: truly, sir, it seem'd
No longer gone than yesterday, that this
Was the sole reason God let me be born
Twenty-five years ago, that I might love
Her, my sweet lady, and be loved by her;
This seem'd so yesterday, to-day death comes,
And is so bitter strong, I cannot see
Why I was born.
                    But as a last request,
I pray you, O kind Clisson, send some man,
Some good man, mind you, to say how I died,
And take my last love to her: fare-you-well,
And may God keep you; I must go now, lest
I grow too sick with thinking on these things;
Likewise my feet are wearied of the earth,
From whence I shall be lifted upright soon.

                                        [*As he goes.*

Ah me! shamed too, I wept at fear of death;
And yet not so, I only wept because
There was no beautiful lady to kiss me
Before I died, and sweetly wish good speed
From her dear lips. O for some lady, though
I saw her ne'er before; Alice, my love,
I do not ask for; Clisson was right kind,
If he had been a woman, I should die
Without this sickness: but I am all wrong,

So wrong, and hopelessly afraid to die.
There, I will go.
　　　　　　　My God! how sick I am,
If only she could come and kiss me now.

The Hotel de la Barde, Bordeaux.
　The Lady Alice de la Barde *looking out of a window into the street.*
No news yet! surely, still he holds his own:
That garde stands well; I mind me passing it
Some months ago; God grant the walls are strong!
I heard some knights say something yestereve,
I tried hard to forget: words far apart
Struck on my heart something like this; one said:
What eh! a Gascon with an English name,
Harpdon? then nought, but afterwards: Poictou.
As one who answers to a question ask'd,
Then carelessly regretful came: No, no.
Whereto in answer loud and eagerly,
One said: Impossible? Christ, what foul play!
And went off angrily; and while thenceforth
I hurried gaspingly afraid, I heard:
Guesclin; Five thousand men-at-arms; Clisson.
My heart misgives me it is all in vain
I send these succours; and in good time there
Their trumpet sounds: ah! here they are; good knights,
God up in Heaven keep you.
　　　　　　　　　　If they come
And find him prisoner, for I can't believe
Guesclin will slay him, even though they storm.
The last horse turns the corner.
　　　　　　　　　　　God in Heaven!
What have I got to thinking of at last!
That thief I will not name is with Guesclin,
Who loves him for his lands. My love! my love!
O, if I lose you after all the past,
What shall I do?
　　　　　　　I cannot bear the noise
And light street out there, with this thought alive,
Like any curling snake within my brain;
Let me just hide my head within these soft
Deep cushions, there to try and think it out.
　　　　　　　　　　[Lying in the window-seat.

I cannot hear much noise now, and I think
That I shall go to sleep: it all sounds dim
And faint, and I shall soon forget most things;
Yea, almost that I am alive and here;
It goes slow, comes slow, like a big mill-wheel
On some broad stream, with long green weeds a-sway,
And soft and slow it rises and it falls,
Still going onward.
              Lying so, one kiss,
And I should be in Avalon asleep,
Among the poppies, and the yellow flowers;
And they should brush my cheek, my hair being spread
Far out among the stems; soft mice and small
Eating and creeping all about my feet,
Red shod and tired; and the flies should come
Creeping o'er my broad eyelids unafraid;
And there should be a noise of water going,
Clear blue fresh water breaking on the slates,
Likewise the flies should creep: God's eyes! God help!
A trumpet? I will run fast, leap adown
The slippery sea-stairs, where the crabs fight.
                                      Ah!

I was half dreaming, but the trumpet's true;
He stops here at our house. The Clisson arms?
Ah, now for news. But I must hold my heart,
And be quite gentle till he is gone out;
And afterwards: but he is still alive,
He must be still alive.

       Enter a Squire *of* Clisson's.

              Good day, fair sir,
I give you welcome, knowing whence you come.

SQUIRE.

My Lady Alice de la Barde, I come
From Oliver Clisson, knight and mighty lord,
Bringing you tidings: I make bold to hope
You will not count me villain, even if
They wring your heart, nor hold me still in hate;
For I am but a mouthpiece after all,
A mouthpiece, too, of one who wishes well

To you and your's.

ALICE.
Can you talk faster, sir,
Get over all this quicker? fix your eyes
On mine, I pray you, and whate'er you see,
Still go on talking fast, unless I fall,
Or bid you stop.

SQUIRE.
I pray your pardon then,
And, looking in your eyes, fair lady, say
I am unhappy that your knight is dead.
Take heart, and listen! let me tell you all.
We were five thousand goodly men-at-arms,
And scant five hundred had he in that hold:
His rotten sand-stone walls were wet with rain,
And fell in lumps wherever a stone hit;
Yet for three days about the barrier there
The deadly glaives were gather'd, laid across,
And push'd and pull'd; the fourth our engines came;
But still amid the crash of falling walls,
And roar of lombards, rattle of hard bolts,
The steady bow-strings flash'd, and still stream'd out
St. George's banner, and the seven swords,
And still they cried: St. George Guienne! until
Their walls were flat as Jericho's of old,
And our rush came, and cut them from the keep.

ALICE.
Stop, sir, and tell me if you slew him then,
And where he died, if you can really mean
That Peter Harpdon, the good knight, is dead?

SQUIRE.
Fair lady, in the base-court:

ALICE.
What base-court?
What do you talk of? Nay, go on, go on;
'Twas only something gone within my head:
Do you not know, one turns one's head round quick,

And something cracks there with sore pain? go on,
And still look at my eyes.

SQUIRE.
                    Almost alone,
There in the base-court fought he with his sword,
Using his left hand much, more than the wont
Of most knights now-a-days; our men gave back,
For wheresoever he hit a downright blow,
Some one fell bleeding, for no plate could hold
Against the sway of body and great arm;
Till he grew tired, and some man (no! not I,
I swear not I, fair lady, as I live!)
Thrust at him with a glaive between the knees,
And threw him; down he fell, sword undermost;
Many fell on him, crying out their cries,
Tore his sword from him, tore his helm off, and:

ALICE.
Yea, slew him: I am much too young to live,
Fair God, so let me die!
                    You have done well,
Done all your message gently, pray you go,
Our knights will make you cheer; moreover, take
This bag of franks for your expenses.

                                        [*The Squire kneels.*

                    But
You do not go; still looking at my face,
You kneel! what, squire, do you mock me then?
You need not tell me who has set you on,
But tell me only, 'tis a made-up tale.
You are some lover may-be or his friend;
Sir, if you loved me once, or your friend loved,
Think, is it not enough that I kneel down
And kiss your feet? your jest will be right good
If you give in now; carry it too far,
And 'twill be cruel: not yet? but you weep
Almost, as though you loved me; love me then,
And go to Heaven by telling all your sport,
And I will kiss you then with all my heart,
Upon the mouth: O! what can I do then
To move you?

SQUIRE.

Lady fair, forgive me still!
You know I am so sorry, but my tale
Is not yet finish'd:

                So they bound his hands,
And brought him tall and pale to Guesclin's tent,
Who, seeing him, leant his head upon his hand,
And ponder'd somewhile, afterwards, looking up:
Fair dame, what shall I say?

ALICE.

                Yea, I know now,
Good squire, you may go now with my thanks.

SQUIRE.

Yet, lady, for your own sake I say this,
Yea, for my own sake, too, and Clisson's sake.
When Guesclin told him he must be hanged soon,
Within a while he lifted up his head
And spoke for his own life; not crouching, though,
As abjectly afraid to die, nor yet
Sullenly brave as many a thief will die,
Nor yet as one that plays at japes with God:
Few words he spoke; not so much what he said
Moved us, I think, as, saying it, there played
Strange tenderness from that big soldier there
About his pleading; eagerness to live
Because folk loved him, and he loved them back,
And many gallant plans unfinish'd now
For ever. Clisson's heart, which may God bless!
Was moved to pray for him, but all in vain;
Wherefore I bring this message:

                      That he waits,
Still loving you, within the little church
Whose windows, with the one eye of the light
Over the altar, every night behold
The great dim broken walls he strove to keep!

There my Lord Clisson did his burial well.
Now, lady, I will go: God give you rest!

ALICE.

Thank Clisson from me, squire, and farewell!
And now to keep myself from going mad.
Christ! I have been a many times to church,
And, ever since my mother taught me prayers,
Have used them daily, but to-day I wish
To pray another way; come face to face,
O Christ, that I may clasp your knees and pray
I know not what; at any rate come now
From one of many places where you are,
Either in Heaven amid thick angel wings,
Or sitting on the altar strange with gems,
Or high up in the duskness of the apse;
Let us go, You and I, a long way off,
To the little damp, dark, Poitevin church.
While you sit on the coffin in the dark,
Will I lie down, my face on the bare stone
Between your feet, and chatter anything
I have heard long ago. What matters it
So I may keep you there, your solemn face
And long hair even-flowing on each side,
Until you love me well enough to speak,
And give me comfort? yea, till o'er your chin,
And cloven red beard the great tears roll down
In pity for my misery, and I die,
Kissed over by you.
                Eh Guesclin! if I were
Like Countess Mountfort now, that kiss'd the knight,
Across the salt sea come to fight for her:
Ah! just to go about with many knights,
Wherever you went, and somehow on one day,
In a thick wood to catch you off your guard,
Let you find, you and your some fifty friends,
Nothing but arrows wheresoe'er you turn'd,
Yea, and red crosses, great spears over them;
And so, between a lane of my true men,
To walk up pale and stern and tall, and with
My arms on my surcoat, and his therewith,
And then to make you kneel, O knight Guesclin;
And then: alas! alas! when all is said,
What could I do but let you go again,

Being pitiful woman? I get no revenge,
Whatever happens; and I get no comfort:
I am but weak, and cannot move my feet,
But as men bid me.

                       Strange I do not die.
Suppose this has not happen'd after all?
I will lean out again and watch for news.

I wonder how long I can still feel thus,
As though I watch'd for news, feel as I did
Just half-an-hour ago, before this news.
How all the street is humming, some men sing,
And some men talk; some look up at the house,
Then lay their heads together and look grave:
Their laughter pains me sorely in the heart;
Their thoughtful talking makes my head turn round:
Yea, some men sing, what is it then they sing?
Eh? Launcelot, and love and fate and death:
They ought to sing of him who was as wight
As Launcelot or Wade, and yet avail'd
Just nothing, but to fail and fail and fail,
And so at last to die and leave me here,
Alone and wretched; yea, perhaps they will,
When many years are past, make songs of us:
God help me, though, truly I never thought
That I should make a story in this way,
A story that his eyes can never see.

                                      [One sings from outside.]

      Therefore be it believed
      Whatsoever he grieved,
      When his horse was relieved,
          This Launcelot,

      Beat down on his knee,
      Right valiant was he
      God's body to see,
          Though he saw it not.

      Right valiant to move,
      But for his sad love
      The high God above
          Stinted his praise.

Yet so he was glad
That his son, Lord Galahad,
That high joyaunce had
    All his life-days.

Sing we therefore then
Launcelot's praise again,
For he wan crownés ten,
    If he wan not twelve.

To his death from his birth
He was mickle of worth,
Lay him in the cold earth,
    A long grave ye may delve.

Omnes homines benedicite!
This last fitte ye may see,
All men pray for me
Who made this history
Cunning and fairly.

Rapunzel

THE PRINCE,
being in the wood near the tower, in the evening.

I could not even think
  What made me weep that day,
When out of the council-hall
  The courtiers pass'd away, —

THE WITCH.

  Rapunzel, Rapunzel,
  Let down your hair!

RAPUNZEL.

Is it not true that every day
She climbeth up the same strange way,
Her scarlet cloak spread broad and gay,
    Over my golden hair?

THE PRINCE.

And left me there alone,
  To think on what they said:
'Thou art a king's own son,
  'Tis fit that thou should'st wed.'

THE WITCH.

  Rapunzel, Rapunzel,
  Let down your hair!

RAPUNZEL.

When I undo the knotted mass,
Fathoms below the shadows pass
Over my hair along the grass.
    O my golden hair!

THE PRINCE.

I put my armour on,
  Thinking on what they said:
'Thou art a king's own son,
  'Tis fit that thou should'st wed.'

THE WITCH.

  Rapunzel, Rapunzel,
  Let down your hair!

RAPUNZEL.

See on the marble parapet,
I lean my brow, strive to forget
That fathoms below my hair grows wet
  With the dew, my golden hair.

THE PRINCE.

I rode throughout the town,
  Men did not bow the head,
Though I was the king's own son:
  He rides to dream, they said.

THE WITCH.

  Rapunzel, Rapunzel,
  Wind up your hair!

RAPUNZEL.

See on the marble parapet,
The faint red stains with tears are wet;
The long years pass, no help comes yet
  To free my golden hair.

THE PRINCE.

For leagues and leagues I rode,
  Till hot my armour grew,
Till underneath the leaves
  I felt the evening dew.

THE WITCH.

  Rapunzel, Rapunzel,
  Weep through your hair!

RAPUNZEL.

And yet: but I am growing old,
For want of love my heart is cold;
Years pass, the while I loose and fold
    The fathoms of my hair.

THE PRINCE,

in the morning.

I have heard tales of men, who in the night
    Saw paths of stars let down to earth from heaven,
Who followed them until they reach'd the light
    Wherein they dwell, whose sins are all forgiven;

But who went backward when they saw the gate
    Of diamond, nor dared to enter in;
All their life long they were content to wait,
    Purging them patiently of every sin.

I must have had a dream of some such thing,
    And now am just awaking from that dream;
For even in grey dawn those strange words ring
    Through heart and brain, and still I see that gleam.

For in my dream at sunset-time I lay
    Beneath these beeches, mail and helmet off,
Right full of joy that I had come away
    From court; for I was patient of the scoff

That met me always there from day to day,
    From any knave or coward of them all:
I was content to live that wretched way;
    For truly till I left the council-hall,

And rode forth arm'd beneath the burning sun,
    My gleams of happiness were faint and few,
But then I saw my real life had begun,
    And that I should be strong quite well I knew.

For I was riding out to look for love,
    Therefore the birds within the thickets sung,
Even in hot noontide; as I pass'd, above

The elms o'ersway'd with longing towards me hung.

Now some few fathoms from the place where I
   Lay in the beech-wood, was a tower fair,
The marble corners faint against the sky;
   And dreamily I wonder'd what lived there:

Because it seem'd a dwelling for a queen,
   No belfry for the swinging of great bells.
No bolt or stone had ever crush'd the green
   Shafts, amber and rose walls, no soot that tells

Of the Norse torches burning up the roofs,
   On the flower-carven marble could I see;
But rather on all sides I saw the proofs
   Of a great loneliness that sicken'd me;

Making me feel a doubt that was not fear,
   Whether my whole life long had been a dream,
And I should wake up soon in some place, where
   The piled-up arms of the fighting angels gleam;

Not born as yet, but going to be born,
   No naked baby as I was at first,
But an armed knight, whom fire, hate and scorn
   Could turn from nothing: my heart almost burst

Beneath the beeches, as I lay a-dreaming,
   I tried so hard to read this riddle through,
To catch some golden cord that I saw gleaming
   Like gossamer against the autumn blue.

But while I ponder'd these things, from the wood
   There came a black-hair'd woman, tall and bold,
Who strode straight up to where the tower stood,
   And cried out shrilly words, whereon behold —

THE WITCH,
from the tower.
Rapunzel, Rapunzel,
Let down your hair!

THE PRINCE.

Ah Christ! it was no dream then, but there stood
  (She comes again) a maiden passing fair,
Against the roof, with face turn'd to the wood,
  Bearing within her arms waves of her yellow hair.

I read my riddle when I saw her stand,
  Poor love! her face quite pale against her hair,
Praying to all the leagues of empty land
  To save her from the woe she suffer'd there.

To think! they trod upon her golden hair
  In the witches' sabbaths; it was a delight
For these foul things, while she, with thin feet bare,
  Stood on the roof upon the winter night,

To plait her dear hair into many plaits,
  And then, while God's eye look'd upon the thing,
In the very likenesses of Devil's bats,
  Upon the ends of her long hair to swing.

And now she stood above the parapet,
  And, spreading out her arms, let her hair flow,
Beneath that veil her smooth white forehead set
  Upon the marble, more I do not know;

Because before my eyes a film of gold
  Floated, as now it floats. O unknown love,
Would that I could thy yellow stair behold,
  If still thou standest the lead roof above!

THE WITCH,
as she passes.
Is there any who will dare
To climb up the yellow stair,
Glorious Rapunzel's golden hair?

THE PRINCE.

If it would please God make you sing again,
  I think that I might very sweetly die,
My soul somehow reach heaven in joyous pain,

My heavy body on the beech-nuts lie.

Now I remember what a most strange year,
   Most strange and awful, in the beechen wood
I have pass'd now; I still have a faint fear
   It is a kind of dream not understood.

I have seen no one in this wood except
   The witch and her; have heard no human tones,
But when the witches' revelry has crept
   Between the very jointing of my bones.

Ah! I know now; I could not go away,
   But needs must stop to hear her sing that song
She always sings at dawning of the day.
   I am not happy here, for I am strong,

And every morning do I whet my sword,
   Yet Rapunzel still weeps within the tower,
And still God ties me down to the green sward,
   Because I cannot see the gold stair floating lower.

RAPUNZEL

sings from the tower.
My mother taught me prayers
To say when I had need;
I have so many cares,
That I can take no heed
Of many words in them;
But I remember this:
Christ, bring me to thy bliss.
Mary, maid withouten wem,
Keep me! I am lone, I wis,
Yet besides I have made this
By myself: *Give me a kiss,*
Dear God dwelling up in heaven!
Also: *Send me a true knight,*
Lord Christ, with a steel sword, bright,
Broad, and trenchant; yea, and seven
Spans from hilt to point, O Lord!
And let the handle of his sword
Be gold on silver, Lord in heaven!

Such a sword as I see gleam
Sometimes, when they let me dream.

Yea, besides, I have made this:
Lord, give Mary a dear kiss,
And let gold Michael, who looked down,
When I was there, on Rouen town
From the spire, bring me that kiss
On a lily! Lord do this!

These prayers on the dreadful nights,
When the witches plait my hair,
And the fearfullest of sights
On the earth and in the air,
Will not let me close my eyes,
I murmur often, mix'd with sighs,
That my weak heart will not hold
At some things that I behold.
Nay, not sighs, but quiet groans,
That swell out the little bones
Of my bosom; till a trance
God sends in middle of that dance,
And I behold the countenance
Of Michael, and can feel no more
The bitter east wind biting sore
My naked feet; can see no more
The crayfish on the leaden floor,
That mock with feeler and grim claw.

Yea, often in that happy trance,
Beside the blessed countenance
Of golden Michael, on the spire
Glowing all crimson in the fire
Of sunset, I behold a face,
Which sometime, if God give me grace,
May kiss me in this very place.
Evening in the tower.

RAPUNZEL.

It grows half way between the dark and light;
   Love, we have been six hours here alone:
I fear that she will come before the night,

And if she finds us thus we are undone.

THE PRINCE.

Nay, draw a little nearer, that your breath
　　May touch my lips, let my cheek feel your arm;
Now tell me, did you ever see a death,
　　Or ever see a man take mortal harm?

RAPUNZEL.

Once came two knights and fought with swords below,
　　And while they fought I scarce could look at all,
My head swam so; after, a moaning low
　　Drew my eyes down; I saw against the wall

One knight lean dead, bleeding from head and breast,
　　Yet seem'd it like a line of poppies red
In the golden twilight, as he took his rest,
　　In the dusky time he scarcely seemed dead.

But the other, on his face, six paces off,
　　Lay moaning, and the old familiar name
He mutter'd through the grass, seem'd like a scoff
　　Of some lost soul remembering his past fame.

His helm all dinted lay beside him there,
　　The visor-bars were twisted towards the face,
The crest, which was a lady very fair,
　　Wrought wonderfully, was shifted from its place.

The shower'd mail-rings on the speedwell lay,
　　Perhaps my eyes were dazzled with the light
That blazed in the west, yet surely on that day
　　Some crimson thing had changed the grass from bright

Pure green I love so. But the knight who died
　　Lay there for days after the other went;
Until one day I heard a voice that cried:
　　Fair knight, I see Sir Robert we were sent

To carry dead or living to the king.
　　So the knights came and bore him straight away
On their lance truncheons, such a batter'd thing,

His mother had not known him on that day,

But for his helm-crest, a gold lady fair
   Wrought wonderfully.

THE PRINCE.
                  Ah, they were brothers then,
And often rode together, doubtless where
   The swords were thickest, and were loyal men,

Until they fell in these same evil dreams.

RAPUNZEL.
   Yea, love; but shall we not depart from hence?
The white moon groweth golden fast, and gleams
   Between the aspens stems; I fear, and yet a sense

Of fluttering victory comes over me,
   That will not let me fear aright; my heart,
Feel how it beats, love, strives to get to thee;
   I breathe so fast that my lips needs must part;

Your breath swims round my mouth, but let us go.

THE PRINCE.
   I, Sebald, also, pluck from off the staff
The crimson banner; let it lie below,
   Above it in the wind let grasses laugh.

Now let us go, love, down the winding stair,
   With fingers intertwined: ay, feel my sword!
I wrought it long ago, with golden hair
   Flowing about the hilts, because a word,

Sung by a minstrel old, had set me dreaming
   Of a sweet bow'd down face with yellow hair;
Betwixt green leaves I used to see it gleaming,
   A half smile on the lips, though lines of care

Had sunk the cheeks, and made the great eyes hollow;
   What other work in all the world had I,
But through all turns of fate that face to follow?

But wars and business kept me there to die.

O child, I should have slain my brother, too,
    My brother, Love, lain moaning in the grass,
Had I not ridden out to look for you,
    When I had watch'd the gilded courtiers pass

From the golden hall. But it is strange your name
    Is not the same the minstrel sung of yore;
You call'd it Rapunzel, 'tis not the name.
    See, love, the stems shine through the open door.
Morning in the woods.

RAPUNZEL.

O love! me and my unknown name you have well won;
    The witch's name was Rapunzel: eh! not so sweet?
No! but is this real grass, love, that I tread upon?
    What call they these blue flowers that lean across my feet?

THE PRINCE.

Dip down your dear face in the dewy grass, O love!
    And ever let the sweet slim harebells, tenderly hung,
Kiss both your parted lips; and I will hang above,
    And try to sing that song the dreamy harper sung.

    He sings.

        'Twixt the sunlight and the shade
        Float up memories of my maid:
                God, remember Guendolen!

        Gold or gems she did not wear,
        But her yellow rippled hair,
                Like a veil, hid Guendolen!

        'Twixt the sunlight and the shade,
        My rough hands so strangely made,
                Folded Golden Guendolen.

        Hands used to grip the sword-hilt hard,
        Framed her face, while on the sward
                Tears fell down from Guendolen.

Guendolen now speaks no word,
Hands fold round about the sword:
          Now no more of Guendolen.

Only 'twixt the light and shade
Floating memories of my maid
          Make me pray for Guendolen.

GUENDOLEN.

I kiss thee, new-found name! but I will never go:
    Your hands need never grip the hammer'd sword again,
But all my golden hair shall ever round you flow,
    Between the light and shade from Golden Guendolen.

Afterwards, in the Palace.

KING SEBALD.

I took my armour off,
    Put on king's robes of gold;
Over the kirtle green
    The gold fell fold on fold.

THE WITCH,
out of hell.

Guendolen! Guendolen!
One lock of hair!

GUENDOLEN.

I am so glad, for every day
He kisses me much the same way
As in the tower: under the sway
          Of all my golden hair.

KING SEBALD.

We rode throughout the town,
    A gold crown on my head;
Through all the gold-hung streets,
    Praise God! the people said.

THE WITCH.

Gwendolen! Guendolen!

Lend me your hair!

GUENDOLEN.

Verily, I seem like one
Who, when day is almost done,
Through a thick wood meets the sun
   That blazes in her hair.

KING SEBALD.

Yea, at the palace gates,
 Praise God! the great knights said,
For Sebald the high king,
 And the lady's golden head.

THE WITCH.

*Woe is me! Guendolen
Sweeps back her hair.*

GUENDOLEN.

Nothing wretched now, no screams;
I was unhappy once in dreams,
And even now a harsh voice seems
   To hang about my hair.

THE WITCH.

WOE! THAT ANY MAN COULD DARE
TO CLIMB UP THE YELLOW STAIR,
GLORIOUS GUENDOLEN'S GOLDEN HAIR.

Concerning Geffray Teste Noire

And if you meet the Canon of Chimay,
   As going to Ortaise you well may do,
Greet him from John of Castel Neuf, and say
   All that I tell you, for all this is true.

This Geffray Teste Noire was a Gascon thief,
   Who, under shadow of the English name,
Pilled all such towns and countries as were lief
   To King Charles and St. Denis; thought it blame

If anything escaped him; so my lord,
   The Duke of Berry, sent Sir John Bonne Lance,
And other knights, good players with the sword,
   To check this thief, and give the land a chance.

Therefore we set our bastides round the tower
   That Geffray held, the strong thief! like a king,
High perch'd upon the rock of Ventadour,
   Hopelessly strong by Christ! It was mid spring,

When first I joined the little army there
   With ten good spears; Auvergne is hot, each day
We sweated armed before the barrier;
   Good feats of arms were done there often. Eh?

Your brother was slain there? I mind me now,
   A right good man-at-arms, God pardon him!
I think 'twas Geffray smote him on the brow
   With some spiked axe, and while he totter'd, dim

About the eyes, the spear of Alleyne Roux
   Slipped through his camaille and his throat; well, well!
Alleyne is paid now; your name Alleyne too?

Mary! how strange! but this tale I would tell:

For spite of all our bastides, damned Blackhead
    Would ride abroad whene'er he chose to ride,
We could not stop him; many a burgher bled
    Dear gold all round his girdle; far and wide

The villaynes dwelt in utter misery
    'Twixt us and thief Sir Geffray; hauled this way
By Sir Bonne Lance at one time; he gone by,
    Down comes this Teste Noire on another day.

And therefore they dig up the stone, grind corn,
    Hew wood, draw water, yea, they lived, in short,
As I said just now, utterly forlorn,
    Till this our knave and blackhead was out-fought.

So Bonne Lance fretted, thinking of some trap
    Day after day, till on a time he said:
John of Newcastle, if we have good hap,
    We catch our thief in two days. How? I said.

Why, Sir, to-day he rideth out again,
    Hoping to take well certain sumpter mules
From Carcassonne, going with little train,
    Because, forsooth, he thinketh us mere fools;

But if we set an ambush in some wood,
    He is but dead: so, Sir, take thirty spears
To Verville forest, if it seem you good.
    Then felt I like the horse in Job, who hears

The dancing trumpet sound, and we went forth;
    And my red lion on the spear-head flapped,
As faster than the cool wind we rode north,
    Towards the wood of Verville; thus it happed.

We rode a soft pace on that day, while spies
    Got news about Sir Geffray: the red wine
Under the road-side bush was clear; the flies,
    The dragon-flies I mind me most, did shine

In brighter arms than ever I put on;
  So: Geffray, said our spies, would pass that way
Next day at sundown: then he must be won;
  And so we enter'd Verville wood next day,

In the afternoon; through it the highway runs,
  'Twixt copses of green hazel, very thick,
And underneath, with glimmering of suns,
  The primroses are happy; the dews lick

The soft green moss: 'Put cloths about your arms,
  Lest they should glitter; surely they will go
In a long thin line, watchful for alarms,
  With all their carriages of booty; so,

Lay down my pennon in the grass: Lord God.
  What have we lying here? will they be cold,
I wonder, being so bare, above the sod,
  Instead of under? This was a knight too, fold

Lying on fold of ancient rusted mail;
  No plate at all, gold rowels to the spurs,
And see the quiet gleam of turquoise pale
  Along the ceinture; but the long time blurs

Even the tinder of his coat to nought,
  Except these scraps of leather; see how white
The skull is, loose within the coif! He fought
  A good fight, maybe, ere he was slain quite.

No armour on the legs too; strange in faith!
  A little skeleton for a knight, though: ah!
This one is bigger, truly without scathe
  His enemies escaped not! ribs driven out far;

That must have reach'd the heart, I doubt: how now,
  What say you, Aldovrand, a woman? why?'
Under the coif a gold wreath on the brow,
  Yea, see the hair not gone to powder, lie,

Golden, no doubt, once: yea, and very small,
  This for a knight; but for a dame, my lord,

These loose-hung bones seem shapely still, and tall.
   Didst ever see a woman's bones, my Lord?

Often, God help me! I remember when
   I was a simple boy, fifteen years old,
The Jacquerie froze up the blood of men
   With their fell deeds, not fit now to be told.

God help again! we enter'd Beauvais town,
   Slaying them fast, whereto I help'd, mere boy
As I was then; we gentles cut them down,
   These burners and defilers, with great joy.

Reason for that, too, in the great church there
   These fiends had lit a fire, that soon went out,
The church at Beauvais being so great and fair:
   My father, who was by me, gave a shout

Between a beast's howl and a woman's scream,
   Then, panting, chuckled to me: 'John, look! look!
Count the dames' skeletons!' From some bad dream
   Like a man just awaked, my father shook;

And I, being faint with smelling the burnt bones,
   And very hot with fighting down the street,
And sick of such a life, fell down, with groans
   My head went weakly nodding to my feet.

— An arrow had gone through her tender throat,
   And her right wrist was broken; then I saw
The reason why she had on that war-coat,
   Their story came out clear without a flaw;

For when he knew that they were being waylaid,
   He threw it over her, yea, hood and all;
Whereby he was much hack'd, while they were stay'd
   By those their murderers; many an one did fall

Beneath his arm, no doubt, so that he clear'd
   Their circle, bore his death-wound out of it;
But as they rode, some archer least afear'd
   Drew a strong bow, and thereby she was hit.

Still as he rode he knew not she was dead,
   Thought her but fainted from her broken wrist,
He bound with his great leathern belt: she bled?
   Who knows! he bled too, neither was there miss'd

The beating of her heart, his heart beat well
   For both of them, till here, within this wood,
He died scarce sorry; easy this to tell;
   After these years the flowers forget their blood.

How could it be? never before that day,
   However much a soldier I might be,
Could I look on a skeleton and say
   I care not for it, shudder not: now see,

Over those bones I sat and pored for hours,
   And thought, and dream'd, and still I scarce could see
The small white bones that lay upon the flowers,
   But evermore I saw the lady; she

With her dear gentle walking leading in,
   By a chain of silver twined about her wrists,
Her loving knight, mounted and arm'd to win
   Great honour for her, fighting in the lists.

O most pale face, that brings such joy and sorrow
   Into men's hearts (yea, too, so piercing sharp
That joy is, that it marcheth nigh to sorrow
   For ever, like an overwinded harp).

Your face must hurt me always: pray you now,
   Doth it not hurt you too? seemeth some pain
To hold you always, pain to hold your brow
   So smooth, unwrinkled ever; yea again,

Your long eyes where the lids seem like to drop,
   Would you not, lady, were they shut fast, feel
Far merrier? there so high they will not stop,
   They are most sly to glide forth and to steal

Into my heart; I kiss their soft lids there,

And in green gardens scarce can stop my lips
From wandering on your face, but that your hair
   Falls down and tangles me, back my face slips.

Or say your mouth, I saw you drink red wine
   Once at a feast; how slowly it sank in,
As though you fear'd that some wild fate might twine
   Within that cup, and slay you for a sin.

And when you talk your lips do arch and move
   In such wise that a language new I know
Besides their sound; they quiver, too, with love
   When you are standing silent; know this, too,

I saw you kissing once, like a curved sword
   That bites with all its edge, did your lips lie,
Curled gently, slowly, long time could afford
   For caught-up breathings: like a dying sigh

They gather'd up their lines and went away,
   And still kept twitching with a sort of smile,
As likely to be weeping presently;
   Your hands too, how I watch'd them all the while!

Cry out St. Peter now, quoth Aldovrand;
   I cried, St. Peter! broke out from the wood
With all my spears; we met them hand to hand,
   And shortly slew them; natheless, by the rood,

We caught not Blackhead then, or any day;
   Months after that he died at last in bed,
From a wound pick'd up at a barrier-fray;
   That same year's end a steel bolt in the head,

And much bad living killed Teste Noire at last;
   John Froissart knoweth he is dead by now,
No doubt, but knoweth not this tale just past;
   Perchance then you can tell him what I show.

In my new castle, down beside the Eure,
   There is a little chapel of squared stone,
Painted inside and out; in green nook pure

There did I lay them, every wearied bone;

And over it they lay, with stone-white hands
  Clasped fast together, hair made bright with gold;
This Jaques Picard, known through many lands,
  Wrought cunningly; he's dead now: I am old.

A Good Knight in Prison

SIR GUY,

being in the court of a Pagan castle.

This castle where I dwell, it stands
A long way off from Christian lands,
A long way off my lady's hands,
A long way off the aspen trees,
And murmur of the lime-tree bees.

But down the Valley of the Rose
My lady often hawking goes,
Heavy of cheer; oft turns behind,
Leaning towards the western wind,
Because it bringeth to her mind
Sad whisperings of happy times,
The face of him who sings these rhymes.

King Guilbert rides beside her there,
Bends low and calls her very fair,
And strives, by pulling down his hair,
To hide from my dear lady's ken
The grisly gash I gave him, when
I cut him down at Camelot;
However he strives, he hides it not,
That tourney will not be forgot,
Besides, it is King Guilbert's lot,
Whatever he says she answers not.

Now tell me, you that are in love,
From the king's son to the wood-dove,
Which is the better, he or I?

For this king means that I should die
In this lone Pagan castle, where

The flowers droop in the bad air
On the September evening.

Look, now I take mine ease and sing,
Counting as but a little thing
The foolish spite of a bad king.

For these vile things that hem me in,
These Pagan beasts who live in sin,
The sickly flowers pale and wan,
The grim blue-bearded castellan,
The stanchions half worn-out with rust,
Whereto their banner vile they trust:
Why, all these things I hold them just
As dragons in a missal book,
Wherein, whenever we may look,
We see no horror, yea delight
We have, the colours are so bright;
Likewise we note the specks of white,
And the great plates of burnish'd gold.

Just so this Pagan castle old,
And everything I can see there,
Sick-pining in the marshland air,
I note: I will go over now,
Like one who paints with knitted brow,
The flowers and all things one by one,
From the snail on the wall to the setting sun.

Four great walls, and a little one
That leads down to the barbican,
Which walls with many spears they man,
When news comes to the castellan
Of Launcelot being in the land.

And as I sit here, close at hand
Four spikes of sad sick sunflowers stand;
The castellan with a long wand
Cuts down their leaves as he goes by,
Ponderingly, with screw'd-up eye,
And fingers twisted in his beard.
Nay, was it a knight's shout I heard?

I have a hope makes me afeard:
It cannot be, but if some dream
Just for a minute made me deem
I saw among the flowers there
My lady's face with long red hair,
Pale, ivory-colour'd dear face come,
As I was wont to see her some
Fading September afternoon,
And kiss me, saying nothing, soon
To leave me by myself again;
   Could I get this by longing? vain!

   The castellan is gone: I see
On one broad yellow flower a bee
Drunk with much honey.
                  Christ! again,
Some distant knight's voice brings me pain,
I thought I had forgot to feel,
I never heard the blissful steel
These ten years past; year after year,
Through all my hopeless sojourn here,
No Christian pennon has been near.
Laus Deo! the dragging wind draws on
Over the marshes, battle won,
Knights' shouts, and axes hammering;
Yea, quicker now the dint and ring
Of flying hoofs; ah, castellan,
When they come back count man for man,
Say whom you miss.

THE PAGANS,
from the battlements.
      Mahound to aid!
Why flee ye so like men dismay'd?

THE PAGANS,
from without.
Nay, haste! for here is Launcelot,
Who follows quick upon us, hot
And shouting with his men-at-arms.

SIR GUY.

Also the Pagans raise alarms,
And ring the bells for fear; at last
My prison walls will be well past.

SIR LAUNCELOT,
from outside.

Ho! in the name of the Trinity,
Let down the drawbridge quick to me,
And open doors, that I may see
Guy the good knight!

THE PAGANS,
from the battlements.
Nay, Launcelot,
With mere big words ye win us not.

SIR LAUNCELOT.

Bid Miles bring up la perriere,
And archers clear the vile walls there.
Bring back the notches to the ear,
Shoot well together! God to aid!
These miscreants will be well paid.

Hurrah! all goes together; Miles
Is good to win my lady's smiles
For his good shooting: Launcelot!
On knights apace! this game is hot!

SIR GUY
sayeth afterwards.

I said, I go to meet her now,
And saying so, I felt a blow
From some clench'd hand across my brow,
And fell down on the sunflowers
Just as a hammering smote my ears;
After which this I felt in sooth,
My bare hands throttling without ruth
The hairy-throated castellan;
Then a grim fight with those that ran
To slay me, while I shouted: God

For the Lady Mary! deep I trod
That evening in my own red blood;
Nevertheless so stiff I stood,
That when the knights burst the old wood
Of the castle-doors, I was not dead.

  I kiss the Lady Mary's head,
Her lips, and her hair golden red,
Because to-day we have been wed.

Old Love

You must be very old, Sir Giles,
  I said; he said: Yea, very old!
Whereat the mournfullest of smiles
  Creased his dry skin with many a fold.

They hammer'd out my basnet point
  Into a round salade, he said,
The basnet being quite out of joint,
  Natheless the salade rasps my head.

He gazed at the great fire awhile:
  And you are getting old, Sir John;
(He said this with that cunning smile
  That was most sad) we both wear on;

Knights come to court and look at me,
  With eyebrows up; except my lord,
And my dear lady, none I see
  That know the ways of my old sword.

(My lady! at that word no pang
  Stopp'd all my blood). But tell me, John,
Is it quite true that Pagans hang
  So thick about the east, that on

The eastern sea no Venice flag
  Can fly unpaid for? True, I said,
And in such way the miscreants drag
  Christ's cross upon the ground, I dread

That Constantine must fall this year.
  Within my heart, these things are small;
This is not small, that things outwear

I thought were made for ever, yea, all,

All things go soon or late, I said.
   I saw the duke in court next day;
Just as before, his grand great head
   Above his gold robes dreaming lay,

Only his face was paler; there
   I saw his duchess sit by him;
And she, she was changed more; her hair
   Before my eyes that used to swim,

And make me dizzy with great bliss
   Once, when I used to watch her sit,
Her hair is bright still, yet it is
   As though some dust were thrown on it.

Her eyes are shallower, as though
   Some grey glass were behind; her brow
And cheeks the straining bones show through,
   Are not so good for kissing now.

Her lips are drier now she is
   A great duke's wife these many years,
They will not shudder with a kiss
   As once they did, being moist with tears.

Also her hands have lost that way
   Of clinging that they used to have;
They look'd quite easy, as they lay
   Upon the silken cushions brave

With broidery of the apples green
   My Lord Duke bears upon his shield.
Her face, alas! that I have seen
   Look fresher than an April field,

This is all gone now; gone also
   Her tender walking; when she walks
She is most queenly I well know,
   And she is fair still. As the stalks

Of faded summer-lilies are,
  So is she grown now unto me
This spring-time, when the flowers star
  The meadows, birds sing wonderfully.

I warrant once she used to cling
  About his neck, and kiss'd him so,
And then his coming step would ring
  Joy-bells for her; some time ago.

Ah! sometimes like an idle dream
  That hinders true life overmuch,
Sometimes like a lost heaven, these seem.
  This love is not so hard to smutch.

The Gilliflower of Gold

A golden gilliflower to-day
I wore upon my helm alway,
And won the prize of this tourney.
Hah! hah! la belle jaune giroflée.

However well Sir Giles might sit,
His sun was weak to wither it,
Lord Miles's blood was dew on it:
Hah! hah! la belle jaune giroflée.

Although my spear in splinters flew,
From John's steel-coat, my eye was true;
I wheel'd about, and cried for you,
Hah! hah! la belle jaune giroflée.

Yea, do not doubt my heart was good,
Though my sword flew like rotten wood,
To shout, although I scarcely stood,
Hah! hah! la belle jaune giroflée.

My hand was steady too, to take
My axe from round my neck, and break
John's steel-coat up for my love's sake.
Hah! hah! la belle jaune giroflée.

When I stood in my tent again,
Arming afresh, I felt a pain
Take hold of me, I was so fain,
Hah! hah! la belle jaune giroflée.

To hear: *Honneur aux fils des preux!*
Right in my ears again, and shew
The gilliflower blossom'd new.

Hah! hah! la belle jaune giroflée.

The Sieur Guillaume against me came,
His tabard bore three points of flame
From a red heart: with little blame,
  Hah! hah! la belle jaune giroflée.

Our tough spears crackled up like straw;
He was the first to turn and draw
His sword, that had nor speck nor flaw;
  Hah! hah! la belle jaune giroflée.

But I felt weaker than a maid,
And my brain, dizzied and afraid,
Within my helm a fierce tune play'd,
  Hah! hah! la belle jaune giroflée.

Until I thought of your dear head,
Bow'd to the gilliflower bed,
The yellow flowers stain'd with red;
  Hah! hah! la belle jaune giroflée.

Crash! how the swords met: *giroflée!*
The fierce tune in my helm would play,
La belle! la belle! jaune giroflée!
  Hah! hah! la belle jaune giroflée.

Once more the great swords met again:
"La belle! la belle!" but who fell then?
Le Sieur Guillaume, who struck down ten;
  Hah! hah! la belle jaune giroflée.

And as with mazed and unarm'd face,
Toward my own crown and the Queen's place,
They led me at a gentle pace.
  Hah! hah! la belle jaune giroflée.

I almost saw your quiet head
Bow'd o'er the gilliflower bed,
The yellow flowers stain'd with red.
  Hah! hah! la belle jaune giroflée.

Shameful Death

There were four of us about that bed;
  The mass-priest knelt at the side,
I and his mother stood at the head,
  Over his feet lay the bride;
We were quite sure that he was dead,
  Though his eyes were open wide.

He did not die in the night,
  He did not die in the day,
But in the morning twilight
  His spirit pass'd away,
When neither sun nor moon was bright,
  And the trees were merely grey.

He was not slain with the sword,
  Knight's axe, or the knightly spear,
Yet spoke he never a word
  After he came in here;
I cut away the cord
  From the neck of my brother dear.

He did not strike one blow,
  For the recreants came behind,
In a place where the hornbeams grow,
  A path right hard to find,
For the hornbeam boughs swing so,
  That the twilight makes it blind.

They lighted a great torch then,
  When his arms were pinion'd fast,
Sir John the knight of the Fen,
  Sir Guy of the Dolorous Blast,
With knights threescore and ten,

Hung brave Lord Hugh at last.

I am threescore and ten,
  And my hair is all turn'd grey,
But I met Sir John of the Fen
  Long ago on a summer day,
And am glad to think of the moment when
  I took his life away.

I am threescore and ten,
  And my strength is mostly pass'd,
But long ago I and my men,
  When the sky was overcast,
And the smoke roll'd over the reeds of the fen,
  Slew Guy of the Dolorous Blast.

And now, knights all of you,
  I pray you pray for Sir Hugh,
A good knight and a true,
  And for Alice, his wife, pray too.

The Eve of Crecy

Gold on her head, and gold on her feet,
And gold where the hems of her kirtle meet,
And a golden girdle round my sweet;
    Ah! qu'elle est belle La Marguerite.

Margaret's maids are fair to see,
Freshly dress'd and pleasantly;
Margaret's hair falls down to her knee;
    Ah! qu'elle est belle La Marguerite.

If I were rich I would kiss her feet;
I would kiss the place where the gold hems meet,
And the golden girdle round my sweet:
    Ah! qu'elle est belle La Marguerite.

Ah me! I have never touch'd her hand;
When the arriere-ban goes through the land,
Six basnets under my pennon stand;
    Ah! qu'elle est belle La Marguerite.

And many an one grins under his hood:
Sir Lambert du Bois, with all his men good,
Has neither food nor firewood;
    Ah! qu'elle est belle La Marguerite.

If I were rich I would kiss her feet,
And the golden girdle of my sweet,
And thereabouts where the gold hems meet;
    Ah! qu'elle est belle La Marguerite.

Yet even now it is good to think,
While my few poor varlets grumble and drink
In my desolate hall, where the fires sink,

Ah! qu'elle est belle La Marguerite.

Of Margaret sitting glorious there,
In glory of gold and glory of hair,
And glory of glorious face most fair;
    Ah! qu'elle est belle La Marguerite.

Likewise to-night I make good cheer,
Because this battle draweth near:
For what have I to lose or fear?
    Ah! qu'elle est belle La Marguerite.

For, look you, my horse is good to prance
A right fair measure in this war-dance,
Before the eyes of Philip of France;
    Ah! qu'elle est belle La Marguerite.

And sometime it may hap, perdie,
While my new towers stand up three and three,
And my hall gets painted fair to see,
    Ah! qu'elle est belle La Marguerite.

That folks may say: Times change, by the rood,
For Lambert, banneret of the wood,
Has heaps of food and firewood;
    Ah! qu'elle est belle La Marguerite;

And wonderful eyes, too, under the hood
Of a damsel of right noble blood.
St. Ives, for Lambert of the Wood!
    Ah! qu'elle est belle La Marguerite.

The Judgment of God

Swerve to the left, son Roger, he said,
    When you catch his eyes through the helmet-slit,
Swerve to the left, then out at his head,
    And the Lord God give you joy of it!

The blue owls on my father's hood
    Were a little dimm'd as I turn'd away;
This giving up of blood for blood
    Will finish here somehow to-day.

So, when I walk'd out from the tent,
    Their howling almost blinded me;
Yet for all that I was not bent
    By any shame. Hard by, the sea

Made a noise like the aspens where
    We did that wrong, but now the place
Is very pleasant, and the air
    Blows cool on any passer's face.

And all the wrong is gather'd now
    Into the circle of these lists:
Yea, howl out, butchers! tell me how
    His hands were cut off at the wrists;

And how Lord Roger bore his face
    A league above his spear-point, high
Above the owls, to that strong place
    Among the waters; yea, yea, cry:

What a brave champion we have got!
    Sir Oliver, the flower of all
The Hainault knights! The day being hot,

He sat beneath a broad white pall,

White linen over all his steel;
    What a good knight he look'd! his sword
Laid thwart his knees; he liked to feel
    Its steadfast edge clear as his word.

And he look'd solemn; how his love
    Smiled whitely on him, sick with fear!
How all the ladies up above
    Twisted their pretty hands! so near

The fighting was: Ellayne! Ellayne!
    They cannot love like you can, who
Would burn your hands off, if that pain
    Could win a kiss; am I not true

To you for ever? therefore I
    Do not fear death or anything;
If I should limp home wounded, why,
    While I lay sick you would but sing,

And soothe me into quiet sleep.
    If they spat on the recreant knight,
Threw stones at him, and cursed him deep,
    Why then: what then? your hand would light

So gently on his drawn-up face,
    And you would kiss him, and in soft
Cool scented clothes would lap him, pace
    The quiet room and weep oft, oft

Would turn and smile, and brush his cheek
    With your sweet chin and mouth; and in
The order'd garden you would seek
    The biggest roses: any sin.

And these say: No more now my knight,
    Or God's knight any longer: you,
Being than they so much more white,
    So much more pure and good and true,

Will cling to me for ever; there,
  Is not that wrong turn'd right at last
Through all these years, and I wash'd clean?
  Say, yea, Ellayne; the time is past,

Since on that Christmas-day last year
  Up to your feet the fire crept,
And the smoke through the brown leaves sere
  Blinded your dear eyes that you wept;

Was it not I that caught you then,
  And kiss'd you on the saddle-bow?
Did not the blue owl mark the men
  Whose spears stood like the corn a-row?

This Oliver is a right good knight,
  And must needs beat me, as I fear,
Unless I catch him in the fight,
  My father's crafty way: John, here!

Bring up the men from the south gate,
  To help me if I fall or win,
For even if I beat, their hate
  Will grow to more than this mere grin.

The Little Tower

Up and away through the drifting rain!
Let us ride to the Little Tower again,

Up and away from the council board!
Do on the hauberk, gird on the sword.

The king is blind with gnashing his teeth,
Change gilded scabbard to leather sheath:

Though our arms are wet with the slanting rain,
This is joy to ride to my love again:

I laugh in his face when he bids me yield;
Who knows one field from the other field,

For the grey rain driveth all astray?
Which way through the floods, good carle, I pray

The left side yet! the left side yet!
Till your hand strikes on the bridge parapet.

Yea so: the causeway holdeth good
Under the water? Hard as wood,

Right away to the uplands; speed, good knight!
Seven hours yet before the light.

Shake the wet off on the upland road;
My tabard has grown a heavy load.

What matter? up and down hill after hill;
Dead grey night for five hours still.

The hill-road droppeth lower again,
Lower, down to the poplar plain.

No furlong farther for us to-night,
The Little Tower draweth in sight;

They are ringing the bells, and the torches glare,
Therefore the roofs of wet slate stare.

There she stands, and her yellow hair slantingly
Drifts the same way that the rain goes by.

Who will be faithful to us to-day,
With little but hard glaive-strokes for pay?

The grim king fumes at the council-board:
Three more days, and then the sword;

Three more days, and my sword through his head;
And above his white brows, pale and dead,

A paper crown on the top of the spire;
And for her the stake and the witches' fire.

Therefore though it be long ere day,
Take axe and pick and spade, I pray.

Break the dams down all over the plain:
God send us three more days such rain!

Block all the upland roads with trees;
The Little Tower with no great ease

Is won, I warrant; bid them bring
Much sheep and oxen, everything

The spits are wont to turn with; wine
And wheaten bread, that we may dine

In plenty each day of the siege.
Good friends, ye know me no hard liege;

My lady is right fair, see ye!
Pray God to keep you frank and free.

Love Isabeau, keep goodly cheer;
The Little Tower will stand well here

Many a year when we are dead,
And over it our green and red,

Barred with the Lady's golden head,
From mere old age when we are dead.

The Sailing of the Sword

Across the empty garden-beds,
  When the Sword went out to sea,
I scarcely saw my sisters' heads
  Bowed each beside a tree.
I could not see the castle leads,
  When the Sword went out to sea,

Alicia wore a scarlet gown,
  When the Sword went out to sea,
But Ursula's was russet brown:
  For the mist we could not see
The scarlet roofs of the good town,
  When the Sword went out to sea.

Green holly in Alicia's hand,
  When the Sword went out to sea;
With sere oak-leaves did Ursula stand;
  O! yet alas for me!
I did but bear a peel'd white wand,
  When the Sword went out to sea.

O, russet brown and scarlet bright,
  When the Sword went out to sea,
My sisters wore; I wore but white:
  Red, brown, and white, are three;
Three damozels; each had a knight,
  When the Sword went out to sea.

Sir Robert shouted loud, and said:
  When the Sword went out to sea,
Alicia, while I see thy head,
  What shall I bring for thee?
O, my sweet Lord, a ruby red:

The Sword went out to sea.

Sir Miles said, while the sails hung down,
  When the Sword went out to sea,
O, Ursula! while I see the town,
  What shall I bring for thee?
Dear knight, bring back a falcon brown:
  The Sword went out to sea.

But my Roland, no word he said
  When the Sword went out to sea,
But only turn'd away his head;
  A quick shriek came from me:
Come back, dear lord, to your white maid.
  The Sword went out to sea.

The hot sun bit the garden-beds
  When the Sword came back from sea;
Beneath an apple-tree our heads
  Stretched out toward the sea;
Grey gleam'd the thirsty castle-leads,
  When the Sword came back from sea.

Lord Robert brought a ruby red,
  When the Sword came back from sea;
He kissed Alicia on the head:
  I am come back to thee;
'Tis time, sweet love, that we were wed,
  Now the Sword is back from sea!

Sir Miles he bore a falcon brown,
  When the Sword came back from sea;
His arms went round tall Ursula's gown:
  What joy, O love, but thee?
Let us be wed in the good town,
  Now the Sword is back from sea!

My heart grew sick, no more afraid,
  When the Sword came back from sea;
Upon the deck a tall white maid
  Sat on Lord Roland's knee;
His chin was press'd upon her head,

When the Sword came back from sea!

Spell-Bound

How weary is it none can tell,
  How dismally the days go by!
I hear the tinkling of the bell,
  I see the cross against the sky.

The year wears round to Autumn-tide,
  Yet comes no reaper to the corn;
The golden land is like a bride
  When first she knows herself forlorn;

She sits and weeps with all her hair
  Laid downward over tender hands;
For stainèd silk she hath no care,
  No care for broken ivory wands;

The silver cups beside her stand;
  The golden stars on the blue roof
Yet glitter, though against her hand
  His cold sword presses for a proof

He is not dead, but gone away.
  How many hours did she wait
For me, I wonder? Till the day
  Had faded wholly, and the gate

Clanged to behind returning knights?
  I wonder did she raise her head
And go away, fleeing the lights;
  And lay the samite on her bed,

The wedding samite strewn with pearls:
  Then sit with hands laid on her knees,
Shuddering at half-heard sound of girls

That chatter outside in the breeze?

I wonder did her poor heart throb
    At distant tramp of coming knight?
How often did the choking sob
    Raise up her head and lips? The light,

Did it come on her unawares,
    And drag her sternly down before
People who loved her not? in prayers
    Did she say one name and no more?

And once, all songs they ever sung,
    All tales they ever told to me,
This only burden through them rung:
    O golden love that waitest me!

The days pass on, pass on apace,
    Sometimes I have a little rest
In fairest dreams, when on thy face
    My lips lie, or thy hands are prest

About my forehead, and thy lips
    Draw near and nearer to mine own;
But when the vision from me slips,
    In colourless dawn I lie and moan,

And wander forth with fever'd blood,
    That makes me start at little things,
The blackbird screaming from the wood,
    The sudden whirr of pheasants' wings.

O dearest, scarcely seen by me!
    But when that wild time had gone by,
And in these arms I folded thee,
    Who ever thought those days could die?

Yet now I wait, and you wait too,
    For what perchance may never come;
You think I have forgotten you,
    That I grew tired and went home.

But what if some day as I stood
  Against the wall with strainèd hands,
And turn'd my face toward the wood,
  Away from all the golden lands;

And saw you come with tired feet,
  And pale face thin and wan with care,
And stainèd raiment no more neat,
  The white dust lying on your hair:

Then I should say, I could not come;
  This land was my wide prison, dear;
I could not choose but go; at home
  There is a wizard whom I fear:

He bound me round with silken chains
  I could not break; he set me here
Above the golden-waving plains,
  Where never reaper cometh near.

And you have brought me my good sword,
  Wherewith in happy days of old
I won you well from knight and lord;
  My heart upswells and I grow bold.

But I shall die unless you stand,
  Half lying now, you are so weak,
Within my arms, unless your hand
  Pass to and fro across my cheek.

The Wind

Ah! no, no, it is nothing, surely nothing at all,
Only the wild-going wind round by the garden-wall,
For the dawn just now is breaking, the wind beginning to fall.

Wind, wind! thou art sad, art thou kind?
Wind, wind, unhappy! thou art blind,
Yet still thou wanderest the lily-seed to find.

So I will sit, and think and think of the days gone by,
Never moving my chair for fear the dogs should cry,
Making no noise at all while the flambeau burns awry.

For my chair is heavy and carved, and with sweeping green behind
It is hung, and the dragons thereon grin out in the gusts of the wind;
On its folds an orange lies, with a deep gash cut in the rind.

Wind, wind! thou art sad, art thou kind?
Wind, wind, unhappy! thou art blind,
still thou wanderest the lily-seed to find.

If I move my chair it will scream, and the orange will roll out afar,
And the faint yellow juice ooze out like blood from a wizard's jar;
And the dogs will howl for those who went last month to the war.

Wind, wind! thou art sad, art thou kind?
Wind, wind, unhappy! thou art blind,
Yet still thou wanderest the lily-seed to find.

So I will sit and think of love that is over and past,
O, so long ago! Yes, I will be quiet at last:
Whether I like it or not, a grim half-slumber is cast

Over my worn old brains, that touches the roots of my heart,

And above my half-shut eyes, the blue roof 'gins to part,
And show the blue spring sky, till I am ready to start

From out of the green-hung chair; but something keeps me still,
And I fall in a dream that I walk'd with her on the side of a hill,
Dotted, for was it not spring? with tufts of the daffodil.

> *Wind, wind! thou art sad, art thou kind?*
> *Wind, wind, unhappy! thou art blind,*
> *Yet still thou wanderest the lily-seed to find.*

And Margaret as she walk'd held a painted book in her hand;
Her finger kept the place; I caught her, we both did stand
Face to face, on the top of the highest hill in the land.

> *Wind, wind! thou art sad, art thou kind?*
> *Wind, wind, unhappy! thou art blind,*
> *Yet still thou wanderest the lily-seed to find.*

I held to her long bare arms, but she shudder'd away from me,
While the flush went out of her face as her head fell back on a tree,
And a spasm caught her mouth, fearful for me to see;

And still I held to her arms till her shoulder touched my mail,
Weeping she totter'd forward, so glad that I should prevail,
And her hair went over my robe, like a gold flag over a sail.

> *Wind, wind! thou art sad, art thou kind?*
> *Wind, wind, unhappy! thou art blind,*
> *Yet still thou wanderest the lily-seed to find.*

I kiss'd her hard by the ear, and she kiss'd me on the brow,
And then lay down on the grass, where the mark on the moss is now,
And spread her arms out wide while I went down below.

> *Wind, wind! thou art sad, art thou kind?*
> *Wind, wind, unhappy! thou art blind,*
> *Yet still thou wanderest the lily-seed to find.*

And then I walk'd for a space to and fro on the side of the hill,
Till I gather'd and held in my arms great sheaves of the daffodil,
And when I came again my Margaret lay there still.

I piled them high and high above her heaving breast,
How they were caught and held in her loose ungirded vest!
But one beneath her arm died, happy so to be prest!

Wind, wind! thou art sad, art thou kind?
Wind, wind, unhappy! thou art blind,
Yet still thou wanderest the lily-seed to find.

Again I turn'd my back and went away for an hour;
She said no word when I came again, so, flower by flower,
I counted the daffodils over, and cast them languidly lower.

Wind, wind! thou art sad, art thou kind?
Wind, wind, unhappy! thou art blind,
Yet still thou wanderest the lily-seed to find.

My dry hands shook and shook as the green gown show'd again,
Clear'd from the yellow flowers, and I grew hollow with pain,
And on to us both there fell from the sun-shower drops of rain.

Wind, wind! thou art sad, art thou kind?
Wind, wind, unhappy! thou art blind,
Yet still thou wanderest the lily-seed to find.

Alas! alas! there was blood on the very quiet breast,
Blood lay in the many folds of the loose ungirded vest,
Blood lay upon her arm where the flower had been prest.

I shriek'd and leapt from my chair, and the orange roll'd out afar,
The faint yellow juice oozed out like blood from a wizard's jar;
And then in march'd the ghosts of those that had gone to the war.

I knew them by the arms that I was used to paint
Upon their long thin shields; but the colours were all grown faint,
And faint upon their banner was Olaf, king and saint.

Wind, wind! thou art sad, art thou kind?
Wind, wind, unhappy! thou art blind,
Yet still thou wanderest the lily-seed to find.

The Blue Closet

THE DAMOZELS

Lady Alice, lady Louise,
Between the wash of the tumbling seas
We are ready to sing, if so ye please;
So lay your long hands on the keys;
                 Sing, *Laudate pueri.*

And ever the great bell overhead
Boom'd in the wind a knell for the dead,
Though no one toll'd it, a knell for the dead.

LADY LOUISE.

Sister, let the measure swell
Not too loud; for you sing not well
If you drown the faint boom of the bell;
              He is weary, so am I.

And ever the chevron overhead
Flapped on the banner of the dead;
(Was he asleep, or was he dead?)

LADY ALICE.

Alice the Queen, and Louise the Queen,
Two damozels wearing purple and green,
Four lone ladies dwelling here
From day to day and year to year;
And there is none to let us go;
To break the locks of the doors below,
Or shovel away the heaped-up snow;
And when we die no man will know
That we are dead; but they give us leave,
Once every year on Christmas-eve,
To sing in the Closet Blue one song;

And we should be so long, so long,
If we dared, in singing; for dream on dream,
They float on in a happy stream;
Float from the gold strings, float from the keys,
Float from the open'd lips of Louise;
But, alas! the sea-salt oozes through
The chinks of the tiles of the Closet Blue;
And ever the great bell overhead
Booms in the wind a knell for the dead,
The wind plays on it a knell for the dead.

They sing all together.

How long ago was it, how long ago,
He came to this tower with hands full of snow?

Kneel down, O love Louise, kneel down! he said,
And sprinkled the dusty snow over my head.

He watch'd the snow melting, it ran through my hair,
Ran over my shoulders, white shoulders and bare.

I cannot weep for thee, poor love Louise,
For my tears are all hidden deep under the seas;

In a gold and blue casket she keeps all my tears,
But my eyes are no longer blue, as in old years;

Yea, they grow grey with time, grow small and dry,
I am so feeble now, would I might die.

And in truth the great bell overhead
Left off his pealing for the dead,
Perchance, because the wind was dead.

Will he come back again, or is he dead?
O! is he sleeping, my scarf round his head?

Or did they strangle him as he lay there,
With the long scarlet scarf I used to wear?

Only I pray thee, Lord, let him come here!

Both his soul and his body to me are most dear.

Dear Lord, that loves me, I wait to receive
Either body or spirit this wild Christmas-eve.

Through the floor shot up a lily red,
With a patch of earth from the land of the dead,
For he was strong in the land of the dead.

What matter that his cheeks were pale,
   His kind kiss'd lips all grey?
O, love Louise, have you waited long?
   O, my lord Arthur, yea.

What if his hair that brush'd her cheek
   Was stiff with frozen rime?
His eyes were grown quite blue again,
   As in the happy time.

O, love Louise, this is the key
   Of the happy golden land!
O, sisters, cross the bridge with me,
   My eyes are full of sand.
What matter that I cannot see,
   If ye take me by the hand?

And ever the great bell overhead,
And the tumbling seas mourned for the dead;
For their song ceased, and they were dead.

The Tune of Seven Towers

No one goes there now:
  For what is left to fetch away
From the desolate battlements all arow,
  And the lead roof heavy and grey?
Therefore, said fair Yoland of the flowers,
This is the tune of Seven Towers.

No one walks there now;
  Except in the white moonlight
The white ghosts walk in a row;
  If one could see it, an awful sight,
Listen! said fair Yoland of the flowers,
This is the tune of Seven Towers.

But none can see them now,
  Though they sit by the side of the moat,
Feet half in the water, there in a row,
  Long hair in the wind afloat.
Therefore, said fair Yoland of the flowers,
This is the tune of Seven Towers.

If any will go to it now,
  He must go to it all alone,
Its gates will not open to any row
  Of glittering spears: will *you* go alone?
Listen! said fair Yoland of the flowers,
This is the tune of Seven Towers.

By my love go there now,
  To fetch me my coif away,
My coif and my kirtle, with pearls arow,
  Oliver, go to-day!
Therefore, said fair Yoland of the flowers,

This is the tune of Seven Towers.

I am unhappy now,
   I cannot tell you why;
If you go, the priests and I in a row
   Will pray that you may not die.
Listen! said fair Yoland of the flowers,
This is the tune of Seven Towers.

If you will go for me now,
   I will kiss your mouth at last;

                                [She sayeth inwardly.]

(The graves stand grey in a row.)
   Oliver, hold me fast!
Therefore, said fair Yoland of the flowers,
This is the tune of Seven Towers.

Golden Wings

Midways of a wallèd garden,
  In the happy poplar land,
  Did an ancient castle stand,
With an old knight for a warden.

Many scarlet bricks there were
  In its walls, and old grey stone;
  Over which red apples shone
At the right time of the year.

On the bricks the green moss grew.
  Yellow lichen on the stone,
  Over which red apples shone;
Little war that castle knew.

Deep green water fill'd the moat,
  Each side had a red-brick lip,
  Green and mossy with the drip
Of dew and rain; there was a boat

Of carven wood, with hangings green
  About the stern; it was great bliss
  For lovers to sit there and kiss
In the hot summer noons, not seen.

Across the moat the fresh west wind
  In very little ripples went;
  The way the heavy aspens bent
Towards it, was a thing to mind.

The painted drawbridge over it
  Went up and down with gilded chains,
  'Twas pleasant in the summer rains

Within the bridge-house there to sit.

There were five swans that ne'er did eat
  The water-weeds, for ladies came
  Each day, and young knights did the same,
And gave them cakes and bread for meat.

They had a house of painted wood,
  A red roof gold-spiked over it,
  Wherein upon their eggs to sit
Week after week; no drop of blood,

Drawn from men's bodies by sword-blows,
  Came ever there, or any tear;
  Most certainly from year to year
'Twas pleasant as a Provence rose.

The banners seem'd quite full of ease,
  That over the turret-roofs hung down;
  The battlements could get no frown
From the flower-moulded cornices.

Who walked in that garden there?
  Miles and Giles and Isabeau,
  Tall Jehane du Castel beau,
Alice of the golden hair,

Big Sir Gervaise, the good knight,
  Fair Ellayne le Violet,
  Mary, Constance fille de fay,
Many dames with footfall light.

Whosoever wander'd there,
  Whether it be dame or knight,
  Half of scarlet, half of white
Their raiment was; of roses fair

Each wore a garland on the head,
  At Ladies' Gard the way was so:
  Fair Jehane du Castel beau
Wore her wreath till it was dead.

Little joy she had of it,
  Of the raiment white and red,
  Or the garland on her head,
She had none with whom to sit

In the carven boat at noon;
  None the more did Jehane weep,
  She would only stand and keep
Saying: He will be here soon!

Many times in the long day
  Miles and Giles and Gervaise passed,
  Holding each some white hand fast,
Every time they heard her say:

Summer cometh to an end,
  Undern cometh after noon;
  Golden wings will be here soon,
What if I some token send?

Wherefore that night within the hall,
  With open mouth and open eyes,
  Like some one listening with surprise,
She sat before the sight of all.

Stoop'd down a little she sat there,
  With neck stretch'd out and chin thrown up,
  One hand around a golden cup;
And strangely with her fingers fair

She beat some tune upon the gold;
  The minstrels in the gallery
  Sung: Arthur, who will never die,
In Avallon he groweth old.

And when the song was ended, she
  Rose and caught up her gown and ran;
  None stopp'd her eager face and wan
Of all that pleasant company.

Right so within her own chamber
  Upon her bed she sat; and drew

Her breath in quick gasps; till she knew
That no man follow'd after her.

She took the garland from her head,
    Loosed all her hair, and let it lie
    Upon the coverlet; thereby
She laid the gown of white and red;

And she took off her scarlet shoon,
    And bared her feet; still more and more
    Her sweet face redden'd; evermore
She murmur'd: He will be here soon;

Truly he cannot fail to know
    My tender body waits him here;
    And if he knows, I have no fear
For poor Jehane du Castel beau.

She took a sword within her hand,
    Whose hilts were silver, and she sung
    Somehow like this, wild words that rung
A long way over the moonlit land:

    Gold wings across the sea!
    Grey light from tree to tree,
    Gold hair beside my knee,
    I pray thee come to me,
    Gold wings!

            The water slips,
        The red-bill'd moorhen dips.
    Sweet kisses on red lips;
    Alas! the red rust grips,
    And the blood-red dagger rips,
    Yet, O knight, come to me!

    Are not my blue eyes sweet?
    The west wind from the wheat
    Blows cold across my feet;
    Is it not time to meet
    Gold wings across the sea?

White swans on the green moat,
Small feathers left afloat
By the blue-painted boat;
Swift running of the stoat,
Sweet gurgling note by note
Of sweet music.

                O gold wings,
Listen how gold hair sings,
And the Ladies Castle rings,
Gold wings across the sea.

I sit on a purple bed,
Outside, the wall is red,
Thereby the apple hangs,
And the wasp, caught by the fangs,

Dies in the autumn night,
And the bat flits till light,
And the love-crazèd knight

Kisses the long wet grass:
The weary days pass,
Gold wings across the sea.

Gold wings across the sea!
Moonlight from tree to tree,
Sweet hair laid on my knee,
O, sweet knight, come to me.

Gold wings, the short night slips,
The white swan's long neck drips,
I pray thee kiss my lips,
Gold wings across the sea!

No answer through the moonlit night;
  No answer in the cold grey dawn;
  No answer when the shaven lawn
Grew green, and all the roses bright.

Her tired feet look'd cold and thin,
  Her lips were twitch'd, and wretched tears,

Some, as she lay, roll'd past her ears,
Some fell from off her quivering chin.

Her long throat, stretched to its full length,
   Rose up and fell right brokenly;
   As though the unhappy heart was nigh
Striving to break with all its strength.

And when she slipp'd from off the bed,
   Her cramp'd feet would not hold her; she
   Sank down and crept on hand and knee,
On the window-sill she laid her head.

There, with crooked arm upon the sill,
   She look'd out, muttering dismally:
   There is no sail upon the sea,
No pennon on the empty hill.

I cannot stay here all alone,
   Or meet their happy faces here,
   And wretchedly I have no fear;
A little while, and I am gone.

Therewith she rose upon her feet,
   And totter'd; cold and misery
   Still made the deep sobs come, till she
At last stretch'd out her fingers sweet,

And caught the great sword in her hand;
   And, stealing down the silent stair,
   Barefooted in the morning air.
And only in her smock, did stand

Upright upon the green lawn grass;
   And hope grew in her as she said:
   I have thrown off the white and red,
And pray God it may come to pass

I meet him; if ten years go by
   Before I meet him; if, indeed,
   Meanwhile both soul and body bleed,
Yet there is end of misery,

And I have hope. He could not come,
   But I can go to him and show
   These new things I have got to know,
And make him speak, who has been dumb.

O Jehane! the red morning sun
   Changed her white feet to glowing gold,
   Upon her smock, on crease and fold,
Changed that to gold which had been dun.

O Miles, and Giles, and Isabeau,
   Fair Ellayne le Violet,
   Mary, Constance fille de fay!
Where is Jehane du Castel beau?

O big Gervaise ride apace!
   Down to the hard yellow sand,
   Where the water meets the land.
This is Jehane by her face.

Why has she a broken sword?
   Mary! she is slain outright;
   Verily a piteous sight;
Take her up without a word!

Giles and Miles and Gervaise there,
   Ladies' Gard must meet the war;
   Whatsoever knights these are,
Man the walls withouten fear!

Axes to the apple-trees,
   Axes to the aspens tall!
   Barriers without the wall
May be lightly made of these.

O poor shivering Isabeau;
   Poor Ellayne le Violet,
   Bent with fear! we miss to-day
Brave Jehane du Castel beau.

O poor Mary, weeping so!

Wretched Constance fille de fay!
Verily we miss to-day
Fair Jehane du Castel beau.

The apples now grow green and sour
Upon the mouldering castle-wall,
Before they ripen there they fall:
There are no banners on the tower,

The draggled swans most eagerly eat
The green weeds trailing in the moat;
Inside the rotting leaky boat
You see a slain man's stiffen'd feet.

The Haystack in the Floods

Had she come all the way for this,
To part at last without a kiss?
Yea, had she borne the dirt and rain
That her own eyes might see him slain
Beside the haystack in the floods?

Along the dripping leafless woods,
The stirrup touching either shoe,
She rode astride as troopers do;
With kirtle kilted to her knee,
To which the mud splash'd wretchedly;
And the wet dripp'd from every tree
Upon her head and heavy hair,
And on her eyelids broad and fair;
The tears and rain ran down her face.
By fits and starts they rode apace,
And very often was his place
Far off from her; he had to ride
Ahead, to see what might betide
When the roads cross'd; and sometimes, when
There rose a murmuring from his men,
Had to turn back with promises.
Ah me! she had but little ease;
And often for pure doubt and dread
She sobb'd, made giddy in the head
By the swift riding; while, for cold,
Her slender fingers scarce could hold
The wet reins; yea, and scarcely, too,
She felt the foot within her shoe
Against the stirrup: all for this,
To part at last without a kiss
Beside the haystack in the floods.

For when they near'd that old soak'd hay,
They saw across the only way
That Judas, Godmar, and the three
Red running lions dismally
Grinn'd from his pennon, under which
In one straight line along the ditch,
They counted thirty heads.

                              So then,
While Robert turn'd round to his men,
She saw at once the wretched end,
And, stooping down, tried hard to rend
Her coif the wrong way from her head,
And hid her eyes; while Robert said:
Nay, love, 'tis scarcely two to one,
At Poictiers where we made them run
So fast: why, sweet my love, good cheer,
The Gascon frontier is so near,
Nought after this.

                         But: O! she said,
My God! my God! I have to tread
The long way back without you; then
The court at Paris; those six men;
The gratings of the Chatelet;
The swift Seine on some rainy day
Like this, and people standing by,
And laughing, while my weak hands try
To recollect how strong men swim.
All this, or else a life with him,
For which I should be damned at last,
Would God that this next hour were past!

He answer'd not, but cried his cry,
St. George for Marny! cheerily;
And laid his hand upon her rein.
Alas! no man of all his train
Gave back that cheery cry again;
And, while for rage his thumb beat fast
Upon his sword-hilt, some one cast
About his neck a kerchief long,
And bound him.

Then they went along
To Godmar; who said: Now, Jehane,
Your lover's life is on the wane
So fast, that, if this very hour
You yield not as my paramour,
He will not see the rain leave off:
Nay, keep your tongue from gibe and scoff
Sir Robert, or I slay you now.

She laid her hand upon her brow,
Then gazed upon the palm, as though
She thought her forehead bled, and: No!
She said, and turn'd her head away,
As there were nothing else to say,
And everything were settled: red
Grew Godmar's face from chin to head:
Jehane, on yonder hill there stands
My castle, guarding well my lands;
What hinders me from taking you,
And doing that I list to do
To your fair wilful body, while
Your knight lies dead?

A wicked smile
Wrinkled her face, her lips grew thin,
A long way out she thrust her chin:
You know that I should strangle you
While you were sleeping; or bite through
Your throat, by God's help: ah! she said,
Lord Jesus, pity your poor maid!
For in such wise they hem me in,
I cannot choose but sin and sin,
Whatever happens: yet I think
They could not make me eat or drink,
And so should I just reach my rest.
Nay, if you do not my behest,
O Jehane! though I love you well,
Said Godmar, would I fail to tell
All that I know? Foul lies, she said.
Eh? lies, my Jehane? by God's head,
At Paris folks would deem them true!

Do you know, Jehane, they cry for you:
Jehane the brown! Jehane the brown!
Give us Jehane to burn or drown!
Eh! gag me Robert! Sweet my friend,
This were indeed a piteous end
For those long fingers, and long feet,
And long neck, and smooth shoulders sweet;
An end that few men would forget
That saw it. So, an hour yet:
Consider, Jehane, which to take
Of life or death!

              So, scarce awake,
Dismounting, did she leave that place,
And totter some yards: with her face
Turn'd upward to the sky she lay,
Her head on a wet heap of hay,
And fell asleep: and while she slept,
And did not dream, the minutes crept
Round to the twelve again; but she,
Being waked at last, sigh'd quietly,
And strangely childlike came, and said:
I will not. Straightway Godmar's head,
As though it hung on strong wires, turn'd
Most sharply round, and his face burn'd.

For Robert, both his eyes were dry,
He could not weep, but gloomily
He seem'd to watch the rain; yea, too,
His lips were firm; he tried once more
To touch her lips; she reached out, sore
And vain desire so tortured them,
The poor grey lips, and now the hem
Of his sleeve brush'd them.

                With a start
Up Godmar rose, thrust them apart;
From Robert's throat he loosed the bands
Of silk and mail; with empty hands
Held out, she stood and gazed, and saw,
The long bright blade without a flaw
Glide out from Godmar's sheath, his hand

In Robert's hair; she saw him bend
Back Robert's head; she saw him send
The thin steel down; the blow told well,
Right backward the knight Robert fell,
And moaned as dogs do, being half dead,
Unwitting, as I deem: so then
Godmar turn'd grinning to his men,
Who ran, some five or six, and beat
His head to pieces at their feet.

Then Godmar turn'd again and said:
So, Jehane, the first fitte is read!
Take note, my lady, that your way
Lies backward to the Chatelet!
She shook her head and gazed awhile
At her cold hands with a rueful smile,
As though this thing had made her mad.

This was the parting that they had
Beside the haystack in the floods.

Two Red Roses across the Moon

There was a lady lived in a hall,
Large of her eyes, and slim and tall;
And ever she sung from noon to noon,
Two red roses across the moon.

There was a knight came riding by
In early spring, when the roads were dry;
And he heard that lady sing at the noon,
Two red roses across the moon.

Yet none the more he stopp'd at all,
But he rode a-gallop past the hall;
And left that lady singing at noon,
Two red roses across the moon.

Because, forsooth, the battle was set,
And the scarlet and blue had got to be met,
He rode on the spur till the next warm noon:
Two red roses across the moon.

But the battle was scatter'd from hill to hill,
From the windmill to the watermill;
And he said to himself, as it near'd the noon,
Two red roses across the moon.

You scarce could see for the scarlet and blue,
A golden helm or a golden shoe:
So he cried, as the fight grew thick at the noon,
Two red roses across the moon!

Verily then the gold bore through
The huddled spears of the scarlet and blue;
And they cried, as they cut them down at the noon,

Two red roses across the moon!

I trow he stopp'd when he rode again
By the hall, though draggled sore with the rain;
And his lips were pinch'd to kiss at the noon
Two red roses across the moon.

Under the may she stoop'd to the crown,
All was gold, there was nothing of brown;
And the horns blew up in the hall at noon,
Two red roses across the moon.

Welland River

Fair Ellayne she walk'd by Welland river,
    Across the lily lee:
O, gentle Sir Robert, ye are not kind
    To stay so long at sea.

Over the marshland none can see
    Your scarlet pennon fair;
O, leave the Easterlings alone,
    Because of my golden hair.

The day when over Stamford bridge
    That dear pennon I see
Go up toward the goodly street,
    'Twill be a fair day for me.

O, let the bonny pennon bide
    At Stamford, the good town,
And let the Easterlings go free,
    And their ships go up and down.

For every day that passes by
    I wax both pale and green,
From gold to gold of my girdle
    There is an inch between.

I sew'd it up with scarlet silk
    Last night upon my knee,
And my heart grew sad and sore to think
    Thy face I'd never see.

I sew'd it up with scarlet silk,
    As I lay upon my bed:
Sorrow! the man I'll never see

That had my maidenhead.

But as Ellayne sat on her window-seat
    And comb'd her yellow hair,
She saw come over Stamford bridge
    The scarlet pennon fair.

As Ellayne lay and sicken'd sore,
    The gold shoes on her feet,
She saw Sir Robert and his men
    Ride up the Stamford street.

He had a coat of fine red gold,
    And a bascinet of steel;
Take note his goodly Collayne sword
    Smote the spur upon his heel.

And by his side, on a grey jennet,
    There rode a fair lady,
For every ruby Ellayne wore,
    I count she carried three.

Say, was not Ellayne's gold hair fine,
    That fell to her middle free?
But that lady's hair down in the street,
    Fell lower than her knee.

Fair Ellayne's face, from sorrow and grief,
    Was waxen pale and green:
That lady's face was goodly red,
    She had but little tene.

But as he pass'd by her window
    He grew a little wroth:
O, why does yon pale face look at me
    From out the golden cloth?

It is some burd, the fair dame said,
    That aye rode him beside,
Has come to see your bonny face
    This merry summer-tide.

But Ellayne let a lily-flower
  Light on his cap of steel:
O, I have gotten two hounds, fair knight,
  The one has served me well;

But the other, just an hour agone,
  Has come from over sea,
And all his fell is sleek and fine,
  But little he knows of me.

Now, which shall I let go, fair knight,
  And which shall bide with me?
O, lady, have no doubt to keep
  The one that best loveth thee.

O, Robert, see how sick I am!
  Ye do not so by me.
Lie still, fair love, have ye gotten harm
  While I was on the sea?

Of one gift, Robert, that ye gave,
  I sicken to the death,
I pray you nurse-tend me, my knight,
  Whiles that I have my breath.

Six fathoms from the Stamford bridge
  He left that dame to stand,
And whiles she wept, and whiles she cursed
  That she ever had taken land.

He has kiss'd sweet Ellayne on the mouth,
  And fair she fell asleep,
And long and long days after that
  Sir Robert's house she did keep.

Riding Together

For many, many days together
   The wind blew steady from the East;
For many days hot grew the weather,
   About the time of our Lady's Feast.

For many days we rode together,
   Yet met we neither friend nor foe;
Hotter and clearer grew the weather,
   Steadily did the East wind blow.

We saw the trees in the hot, bright weather,
   Clear-cut, with shadows very black,
As freely we rode on together
   With helms unlaced and bridles slack.

And often as we rode together,
   We, looking down the green-bank'd stream,
Saw flowers in the sunny weather,
   And saw the bubble-making bream.

And in the night lay down together,
   And hung above our heads the rood,
Or watch'd night-long in the dewy weather,
   The while the moon did watch the wood.

Our spears stood bright and thick together,
   Straight out the banners stream'd behind,
As we gallop'd on in the sunny weather,
   With faces turn'd towards the wind.

Down sank our threescore spears together,
   As thick we saw the pagans ride;
His eager face in the clear fresh weather,

Shone out that last time by my side.

Up the sweep of the bridge we dash'd together,
   It rock'd to the crash of the meeting spears,
Down rain'd the buds of the dear spring weather,
   The elm-tree flowers fell like tears.

There, as we roll'd and writhed together,
   I threw my arms above my head,
For close by my side, in the lovely weather,
   I saw him reel and fall back dead.

I and the slayer met together,
   He waited the death-stroke there in his place,
With thoughts of death, in the lovely weather,
   Gapingly mazed at my madden'd face.

Madly I fought as we fought together;
   In vain: the little Christian band
The pagans drown'd, as in stormy weather,
   The river drowns low-lying land.

They bound my blood-stain'd hands together,
   They bound his corpse to nod by my side:
Then on we rode, in the bright March weather,
   With clash of cymbals did we ride.

We ride no more, no more together;
   My prison-bars are thick and strong,
I take no heed of any weather,
   The sweet Saints grant I live not long.

Father John's War-Song

THE REAPERS.

So many reapers, Father John,
So many reapers and no little son,
To meet you when the day is done,
With little stiff legs to waddle and run?
Pray you beg, borrow, or steal one son.
Hurrah for the corn-sheaves of Father John!

FATHER JOHN.

O maiden Mary, be wary, be wary!
And go not down to the river,
Lest the kingfisher, your evil wisher,
Lure you down to the river,
Lest your white feet grow muddy,
Your red hair too ruddy
With the river-mud so red;
But when you are wed
Go down to the river.
O maiden Mary, be very wary,
And dwell among the corn!
See, this dame Alice, maiden Mary,
Her hair is thin and white,
But she is a housewife good and wary,
And a great steel key hangs bright
From her gown, as red as the flowers in corn;
She is good and old like the autumn corn.

MAIDEN MARY.

This is knight Roland, Father John,
Stark in his arms from a field half-won;
Ask him if he has seen your son:
Roland, lay your sword on the corn,
The piled-up sheaves of the golden corn.

KNIGHT ROLAND.

Why does she kiss me, Father John?
She is my true love truly won!
Under my helm is room for one,
But the molten lead-streams trickle and run
From my roof-tree, burning under the sun;
No corn to burn, we had eaten the corn,
There was no waste of the golden corn.

FATHER JOHN.

Ho, you reapers, away from the corn,
To march with the banner of Father John!

THE REAPERS.

We will win a house for Roland his son,
And for maiden Mary with hair like corn,
As red as the reddest of golden corn.

OMNES.

Father John, you have got a son,
Seven feet high when his helm is on
Pennon of Roland, banner of John,
Star of Mary, march well on.

Sir Giles' War-Song

Ho! is there any will ride with me,
Sir Giles, le bon des barrières?

The clink of arms is good to hear,
The flap of pennons fair to see;
Ho! is there any will ride with me,
Sir Giles, le bon des barrières?

The leopards and lilies are fair to see;
St. George Guienne! right good to hear:
Ho! is there any will ride with me,
Sir Giles, le bon des barrières?

I stood by the barrier,
My coat being blazon'd fair to see;
Ho! is there any will ride with me,
Sir Giles, le bon des barrières?

Clisson put out his head to see,
And lifted his basnet up to hear;
I pull'd him through the bars to *me*,
Sir Giles; le bon des barrières.

Near Avalon

A ship with shields before the sun,
Six maidens round the mast,
A red-gold crown on every one,
A green gown on the last.

The fluttering green banners there
Are wrought with ladies' heads most fair,
And a portraiture of Guenevere
The middle of each sail doth bear.

A ship which sails before the wind,
And round the helm six knights,
Their heaumes are on, whereby, half blind,
They pass by many sights.

The tatter'd scarlet banners there,
Right soon will leave the spear-heads bare.
Those six knights sorrowfully bear,
In all their heaumes some yellow hair.

Praise of My Lady

My lady seems of ivory
Forehead, straight nose, and cheeks that be
Hollow'd a little mournfully.
    Beata mea Domina!

Her forehead, overshadow'd much
By bows of hair, has a wave such
As God was good to make for me.
    Beata mea Domina!

Not greatly long my lady's hair,
Nor yet with yellow colour fair,
But thick and crispèd wonderfully:
    Beata mea Domina!

Heavy to make the pale face sad,
And dark, but dead as though it had
Been forged by God most wonderfully
    Beata mea Domina!

Of some strange metal, thread by thread,
To stand out from my lady's head,
Not moving much to tangle me.
    Beata mea Domina!

Beneath her brows the lids fall slow.
The lashes a clear shadow throw
Where I would wish my lips to be.
    Beata mea Domina!

Her great eyes, standing far apart,
Draw up some memory from her heart,
And gaze out very mournfully;

Beata mea Domina!

So beautiful and kind they are,
But most times looking out afar,
Waiting for something, not for me.
            Beata mea Domina!

I wonder if the lashes long
Are those that do her bright eyes wrong,
For always half tears seem to be
            Beata mea Domina!

Lurking below the underlid,
Darkening the place where they lie hid:
If they should rise and flow for me!
            Beata mea Domina!

Her full lips being made to kiss,
Curl'd up and pensive each one is;
This makes me faint to stand and see.
            Beata mea Domina!

Her lips are not contented now,
Because the hours pass so slow
Towards a sweet time: (pray for me),
            Beata mea Domina!

Nay, hold thy peace! for who can tell?
But this at least I know full well,
Her lips are parted longingly,
            Beata mea Domina!

So passionate and swift to move,
To pluck at any flying love,
That I grow faint to stand and see.
            Beata mea Domina!

Yea! there beneath them is her chin,
So fine and round, it were a sin
To feel no weaker when I see
            Beata mea Domina!

God's dealings; for with so much care
And troublous, faint lines wrought in there,
He finishes her face for me.
    Beata mea Domina!

Of her long neck what shall I say?
What things about her body's sway,
Like a knight's pennon or slim tree
    Beata mea Domina!

Set gently waving in the wind;
Or her long hands that I may find
On some day sweet to move o'er me?
    Beata mea Domina!

God pity me though, if I miss'd
The telling, how along her wrist
The veins creep, dying languidly
    Beata mea Domina!

Inside her tender palm and thin.
Now give me pardon, dear, wherein
My voice is weak and vexes thee.
    Beata mea Domina!

All men that see her any time,
I charge you straightly in this rhyme,
What, and wherever you may be,
    Beata mea Domina!

To kneel before her; as for me,
I choke and grow quite faint to see
My lady moving graciously.
    Beata mea Domina!

Summer Dawn

Pray but one prayer for me 'twixt thy closed lips;
  Think but one thought of me up in the stars.
The summer night waneth, the morning light slips,
    Faint and grey 'twixt the leaves of the aspen, betwixt the
                cloud-bars,
That are patiently waiting there for the dawn:
  Patient and colourless, though Heaven's gold
Waits to float through them along with the sun.
Far out in the meadows, above the young corn,
  The heavy elms wait, and restless and cold
The uneasy wind rises; the roses are dun;
They pray the long gloom through for daylight new born,
Round the lone house in the midst of the corn.
  Speak but one word to me over the corn,
  Over the tender, bow'd locks of the corn.

In Prison

Wearily, drearily,
Half the day long,
Flap the great banners
High over the stone;
Strangely and eerily
Sounds the wind's song,
Bending the banner-poles.

While, all alone,
Watching the loophole's spark,
Lie I, with life all dark,
Feet tether'd, hands fetter'd
Fast to the stone,
The grim walls, square letter'd
With prison'd men's groan.

Still strain the banner-poles
Through the wind's song,
Westward the banner rolls
Over my wrong.

THE END